Gilgamesh

Gilgamesh

JO BANNISTER

A CRIME CLUB BOOK
DOUBLEDAY
NEW YORK   LONDON   TORONTO   SYDNEY   AUCKLAND

A CRIME CLUB BOOK

Published by DOUBLEDAY, a division of Bantam Doubleday Dell Publishing Group, Inc., 666 Fifth Avenue, New York, New York 10103

DOUBLEDAY and the portrayal of a man with a gun are trademarks of Doubleday, a division of Bantam Doubleday Dell Publishing Group, Inc.

Library of Congress Cataloging-in-Publication Data
Bannister, Jo.
  Gilgamesh / Jo Bannister.
      p.   cm.
  "A Crime Club book."
  ISBN 0-385-24934-9
  I. Title.
PR6052.A497G55   1989
823'.914—dc19   88-24078
                                                      CIP

OG

190p.

Gilgamesh

CHAPTER 1

The Dark Horse

I

It was the first really warm evening of the summer. After dinner we repaired to the drawing-room to watch the sun go down over Foxford Wood. Now we were into May, it was in no great hurry but seemed to hang endlessly over The Brink, bleeding pink and golden streamers through the shot-silk sky.

The drawing-room windows were Tudor, the original intricate mullions casting shadows of almost oriental complexity across the floor and up the walls. In the cold hard light of day it was clear that the window frames needed attention, that the floor was sagging and the plaster cracked, but the setting sun gave us all rose-tinted vision.

Besides, pristine or shabby, Foxford was charming—not the biggest, or the grandest, or the oldest, or the most architecturally perfect house I'd ever been in, but far and away the most charming. And besides that, it was the home of two very good friends. Given that Harry was otherwise occupied this evening, I couldn't think of anything I'd rather be doing than sitting in the Tudor window of Foxford's charming, threadbare drawing-room, digesting Ellen Aston's excellent dinner, sipping David Aston's home-pickled wine, and watching the sun leak water-colours through the sky.

From the other window, on the front of the house, I could look down over The Brink and the tiles of our house—mine and Harry's, all but lost among the burgeoning hedgerows a quarter of a mile away—onto Skipley, its first lights out and twinkling dimly, its dark ungracious form lurking in the valley softened by the translucence of the summer evening. It was dark little towns like Skipley, uncompromising in their creation by and dedication to the Industrial Revolution, that gave the Black Country its name. I had never thought to live here or anywhere like here.

But from the window where I sat, my eye travelled along the side of the old brick byre, across David's sand school and then along the swell of The Brink, the angularity of the escarpment blunted by time and clothed in the fertile farmland of the Shires, green and gold with the ripening harvest, to the secret shadowy bluff of the woods and beyond across all of Yeoman England to the borders of Wales. Time and scale seemed as nothing in these closing minutes of the day.

I said, "It doesn't look Harry's going to make it now. I'm sorry, Ellen."

She smiled, untroubled. "I'm sorry too, but it doesn't matter. There'll be another chance. He'd have got here if he could. What was it this time?"

I winced. All our friends knew the risks of inviting my husband anywhere. They didn't even get annoyed when he didn't show, just wondered what had stopped him this time. "A conference in Coventry. Policing the Midlands into the 1990s. In essence, a fifteen-rounds, no-holds-barred, all-in wrestling-match between the Chief Constable and the rest of the force over allocations, priorities, manning levels, and so on. It must have gone the distance."

"Take him some chicken pie for his supper." She went back to the kitchen to make up a doggy-bag. The gesture defined quite neatly the friendship we had developed in the last year: unpretentious, pragmatic and warm. Harry would deem it a real favour that Ellen had sent a piece of her pie in compensation for missing dinner, and I did too.

I said to David, "So what's the next step for the Lester Piggott of the eventing world?"

He grinned, a dry little grin that arched the sandy brow over one green eye. "The eventing world doesn't have any Lester Pig-gotts. The only people who make real money out of it are the feed merchants."

"But the glamour!" I exclaimed, winding him up a little, I admit it.

"Oh yes, there's that," he agreed. "There can be few more glamorous experiences in this world than walking two miles home with your boots full of pondweed in pursuit of a horse that has just up-ended you in two feet of lake water in front of several thousand people. And the TV cameras. Julian Seaman had an interesting cock-up once, and the BBC started 'Grandstand' with it fifty-three consecutive times."

"Well," I said, "if it isn't profitable and it isn't glamorous, you'll hardly care whether you get going to the world championships or not."

"If you believe that," said David, "you'll believe anything."

Actually, apart from Cyril Smith, no one was less likely to be mistaken for Lester Piggott or any flat-race jockey. He was a tall man, as tall as Harry, with long strong limbs and powerful muscles across his shoulders, and he walked like one of his horses, with long, free, mile-eating strides. Sun and wind had bleached his hair and faded his green eyes like an old cowboy's and creased up the skin of his face, and now the eyes and the creases and the broad friendly mouth fell into a happy grin of their own volition.

"The next thing is to finish a couple more events in good shape —in the top four, say, and still with a leg at each corner. The long list will be reduced to a short list after Gatcombe in August, and if we're still on that, we lie, cheat, steal, crawl, and, if absolutely necessary, jump some fences to keep in with the selectors. There'll be a training session, and then they'll announce the team. If we're on it, we celebrate and start worrying in earnest. If not, we make loud remarks in beer tents about how the selectors are related to all the men on the team and having relations with all the women."

The phone rang. David answered it and exchanged greetings; then he put a hand over the mouthpiece and grimaced at me. "It's one of my owners. I owe her a report on her horse, and then we need to talk about what we aim him for next. I'll take it in the study; I have the schedules and my diary and everything in there. Can you give me a moment and then hang up?"

I took the receiver from him. "Don't worry, your home brew is safe with me." It was too. I waited for the click on the line and hung up.

Ellen came back with a tray of coffee and a substantial parcel. "I could put what's left of the wine in," she said doubtfully.

"Serve him right," I agreed.

She giggled. "Yes, it really is pretty vile, isn't it?"

"I hope this works out for David," I said. "He deserves it; he's worked hard."

"They all work hard. There's also a big element of luck: the right horse at the right time. Even then it can all go wrong. Horses come apart easier than most things, and they've a nasty habit of saving a really good big knee or sprained tendon for the week before the big event."

"Hush," I said, glancing uneasily at the ceiling. "Somebody'll hear you."

Ellen shrugged. "It's just another of the risks you take in this business. Everyone has at least one hard-luck story; some people have runs of misfortune you can hardly believe are coincidence. David lost an event once when his horse, which had led after dressage, gone clear across country under the time allowed, and passed the vet next morning, tripped over a Jack Russell and pulled a ligament on its way out to the show-jumping. The disappointments are just part of the game; you have to grin and bear them."

I shuddered. "I don't think I could cope with that sort of uncertainty. Fortunately it doesn't matter, because I couldn't do any of the rest of it either."

"You just have to enyoy it while it lasts and accept that it won't last for ever. All the same, it's hard when the bubble bursts. Do you know the Fanes at Standings, who David bought his horse from?"

I nodded. I knew them a little, the retired colonel and his striking daughter.

"Three or four years ago Sally seemed one of the best young prospects in eventing. She had a good horse that chalked up several good results in a row, a couple of top yards were offering her rides, and the smart money said she'd ride for her country before she was twenty-five. Then the bubble burst. Her good horse ran into some back trouble and had to be rested for a year. She had no young hopeful ready to fill in, and when Pasha was no longer winning big prizes at important events, the owners who'd been so keen on her riding for them lost interest and went courting riders whose names were in this month's papers, not just last month's.

"She never really recovered from that. The next year Pasha was fit again, but he was already past his prime and no one ever offered her another chance on a really good horse. Mostly what she does now is break horses and bring them out as novices; she still competes, but not at David's level, I think mostly it's for fun. It's a nice enough life; she seems to enjoy herself, but it's not what any of us expected for her. That's what it's like, literally not knowing what tomorrow's going to bring. That's what keeps us all glancing over our shoulders and checking our insurance policies."

It was as if a cold air had moved through the room. I had thought my business a shade on the precarious side, but I didn't begin to understand what living dangerously was about. I shook off the momentary oppression. "The horse he got from the Fanes: is that the one they're considering for the world championships?"

"The big bay bastard, that's right. He's the best horse David's ever had, and quite the least likeable."

We drank the coffee. Ellen took a cup to the study. The roseate sun lowered itself slowly onto the ragged head of Foxford Wood, a little like a reluctant fakir trying out a new bed of nails. Against the glowing disc the treetops stood out preternaturally clear and close, like moss seen through a raindrop.

The phone said "ding" as David put it down, but he clearly wasn't finished yet. We could faintly hear him busy behind the thick wall—the rattle of a filing cabinet, then a crack and a clatter as if the books piled high on his desk had all gone flying at once.

"I wish," Ellen said thoughtfully, "that David would tell Mrs. Cooper that her horse will never be better than a decent one-day-eventer, instead of letting her persuade him to enter it for things it isn't up to and then taking out his frustration on the furniture."

We waited for David to return, but patently he was still struggling on the horns of his dilemma. At least he was doing it quietly now. Well, more quietly: a dull clang reached our ears and we both grinned.

After another minute I stood up. "Listen, I'd better make a move. Ellen, it was a lovely dinner, but I'd have been happy to celebrate David's news with a hamburger. I'll just stick my head in on the way past and say goodnight."

I forgot the doggy-bag. Ellen went back for it. I opened the study door. "I'm just on my way, David. Listen, I do wish you every—"

It hadn't been David's books hitting the floor; it had been David. He lay sprawled in front of the desk, his long legs entangled with those of his upturned chair. He was mostly on his face, and the breeze through the French window stirred his sandy hair. There was a round mark, black and red, in the small of his back.

"Jesus Christ!" Shock kicked me back nearly twenty years to when I was a young casualty officer faced with my first gunshot wound. Now as then my first thought was not for what had happened but for whether I'd be able to cope. Now, as then, I had to push myself to take the first step towards assuming responsibility for the hurt and hurting man.

I dropped on my knees beside him. "David, can you hear me?"

He wasn't unconscious, but nor was he that far off. His eyes were stretched, glazed and vacant. The fine dew of sweat on his face was nothing to do with the warmth of the evening. His skin felt cool to the touch.

His eyes crept round to my face. "Clio?" His voice was weak and breathy, and he sounded surprised to see me. "What happened?"

"An accident," I lied. "Lie still, love, we'll soon sort you out."

There was virtually no bleeding from the hole in his back. I passed my hand under his belly but found no evidence of an exit wound. If he wasn't bleeding, I didn't want to move him any more than that.

I yelled, "Ellen, get in here." My voice cracked in a not wholly professional fashion. But then, bullet wounds weren't my profession any more, or only in a way.

I couldn't spare the time to watch her face when she came in with Harry's supper and saw her husband lying there like a felled tree. I heard her gasp, but by then I was on the phone.

In gaps while I was put through, I said, "Get a blanket. Nothing too heavy, but we need to keep him warm. Hold his hand, but don't let him try to move. It's all right, the ambulance will be here in ten minutes." In fact, the ambulance was there in five, but it still wasn't all right.

With the emergency services on their way, I went back to my patient. There wasn't that much I could do for him. He needed no help with his breathing, which was free enough if stressed and shallow, and his pulse was rapid and thready but essentially competent. I didn't think there was significant bleeding inside or out. I didn't think his life was in any immediate danger. For all my experience and expertise, I couldn't do more in that particular situation than anyone could have done: keep him warm and comfortable until the ambulance arrived, and reassure his wife, crouching white-faced over his long, still, tumbled body.

And try to fight back the rage that was growing in me, the towering rage at what had been done to my friend while he sat defenceless and unsuspecting with his back to the window, the impotent fury at what had been done to him in his own home, on one of the best days of his life, while I had sat only the width of a thick wall away but quite powerless to prevent it.

There would be a time for anger, but not now with the man still lying brokenly on his study carpet and his wife looking in shock for some kind of explanation, which I didn't have, or help which I couldn't offer. Everything I could do I had already done; all that was left to do was wait.

I have never been good at waiting.

I started to my feet. "Stay here, Ellen. I'll go meet the ambulance, bring them round the side. Try not to be frightened; it doesn't look too bad." It was the truth but not the whole truth. It didn't look too bad for a gunshot wound to a man's back, but there are no good ones.

I went out through the French window and jogged round the side of the house. To be honest, it wasn't the ambulance I was looking for. To be entirely honest, I don't know what I was looking for. If I'd thought there was any danger of meeting the gunman in the dusk, I'd have found an urgent reason to stay with my injured friend and lock all the doors and windows as well.

But I did see him. At least, I saw—momentarily silhouetted against the glow of the dying sunset—a figure I took to be the man who had shot my friend David through his own French windows, and he was bent low and scuttling across the top end of the sand school towards the thick thorn hedge between the cross-country field and the wood.

It was only a moment before the dark figure disappeared against the greater darkness of that big old hedge, and could have gone up the line of it towards the wood or round the back of the byre and up through the yard towards the lane. But for that moment my eye held frozen a picture of a bulky, shapeless form running bent almost double over the long, thin thing I took to be the gun. I opened my mouth to shout after him, but only a whisper came out. I couldn't tell if he knew I was there or not. After a moment, I could no longer tell if he was there or not.

And after only a minute longer I heard the two-tone siren of the ambulance coming up the hill from Skipley, growing swiftly from faint beginnings to a banshee howl as it cornered the gatepost. It crashed to a halt with a spitting of gravel and two men jumped out with a stretcher.

Ellen went with the ambulance. I stayed behind to talk to the police.

The first car arrived just behind the ambulance. John Martin was the senior detective. We greeted one another with the slightly embarrassed rectitude of two people who last met in a singing conga line at Skipley Policemen's Ball.

"Harry wasn't back, then?"

"We took a swing round your house on the way up. He'd just got in; he'll be along in a minute." He looked round the study, not in microscopic detail with a magnifying glass but by pivoting slowly on his heel in the centre. I saw him register the fallen chair and the open window. He was the only policeman I ever knew who didn't look at least as much like a policeman in plain clothes as he had in uniform. With his wide, permanently wrinkled forehead and nondescript little moustache, he looked exactly like a local-authority parks superintendent.

"What happened?"

I told him what I had heard and what I had seen. Even if the crouched and running figure was indeed the gunman, it amounted to very little. I had heard a rattle, a crack, a clatter, and a clang, and seen a dim figure run for the cover of the hedge.

"Was the French window open before the shooting?"

"I don't know."

"Did they speak, or did he fire first?"

"I didn't hear."

"Is there anything missing, do you know?"

"I don't, John, I'm sorry. I've been in here before, but I couldn't say—"

But there was something different, even though it took me a minute to realise what. There was too much wall showing. "There used to be a picture over the desk there. An old brown thing—a horse, of course. I couldn't swear it was there this evening. They may have taken it down, for cleaning or something. You'd need to ask Ellen."

"A picture. About how big?" He watched with growing scepticism while my outstretched arms sketched dimensions. "I imagine you'd have noticed if your running man had been carrying something that size."

"I would, and he wasn't. Listen, shouldn't you set up roadblocks or something?"

"I should," he said heavily. "And I have. How long after the shooting did we get your call?"

"It must have been a few minutes. Neither of us—Ellen or me—realised it was a shot. It was only when I went to leave that I found—" I swallowed. "But if the man I saw was the gunman, he was still here after I called. I'm sorry, I don't know which way he went."

"Never mind; by then we had cars in the area. They may have him boxed up, even if they don't know it yet. If they find his car, we'll be getting somewhere. I don't suppose you heard a car?"

"Sorry."

The gravel spat again and it was Harry. He looked as though he'd had a hard day, and it wasn't over yet. "Are you all right?"

"I'm fine," I said somewhat testily. "It wasn't me that got shot."

He checked with John Martin what had already been done and discovered. He had me go over my meagre contribution again. Then he nodded. "OK. Well, I don't think there's much more you can do here. Do you want to go on down to the hospital? I dare say Ellen could use the company."

Outside the last of the sun had gone, and as I walked to my car, the last of the afterlight died out of the sky. We looked as if we were in for a long, dark night.

II

Skipley General Hospital squatted in brick and Nissen-hut confusion at the foot of The Brink, beside the ring road. As I drove down the hill the street-lights greeted me, twinkling pink and prettily in the dip. It was the closest Skipley ever got to picturesque.

The girl at reception remembered me. "Dr. Rees, isn't it?"

It wasn't any more, on either count, but I didn't trouble to update her. "I'm looking for Mrs. Aston. Her husband was admitted with a gunshot wound."

She nodded. "She's in matron's office." Since the Sex Discrimination Act, hospitals don't have matrons; they have chief nursing officers and the like, but chief nursing officers always live in matron's office. "There's a policeman with her."

There was something very faintly objectionable about the way she said it. I think she'd remembered that last time I was in this hospital I got their pathologist arrested. I found a condescending little smile and ran it up the flagpole. "That's all right, I'm broadminded."

Ellen looked up when I opened the door, with that same compound of hope and fear that used to tear me up when I worked in hospitals. She thought I was bringing her news, and half of her wanted it quickly in case it was good and the other half didn't want it at all for fear it was bad.

"It's only me, Ellen." I went quickly and sat down beside her.

She had half risen at the sound of the door, twisting up out of her seat. Now she dropped back into it, her hands falling into her lap, her head bowed, her shoulders folded round her breasts. Her fair hair was tangled, her face a desolation, bereft even of tears. It seemed incredible that only an hour had passed since she and I had been giggling over David's wine.

Sergeant Ross nodded me an acknowledgement from the desk on which he had parked his posterior. He was the ideal relative-sitter, a policeman with all the vital attributes of a teddy bear.

I said to him, "Any news?"

He shook his head. "He's in theatre at the moment. We're just waiting to hear how he got on."

I nodded. There was no point in probing for details with Ellen there. The full picture would come later. For the moment, I knew all I needed to do my job, which was not David but his wife. I took one of her hands and held it, saying nothing. After a few minutes she turned towards me, also without speaking, and buried her face in my sleeve, and clung to my arm as to a lifeline, while great racking sobs tore out of her throat.

I held her tight while the storm peaked and began to pass. After that we just leaned together on the settee, our arms round one another, because the comfort of touch was all that either of us had to offer. For Ellen it was little enough. She was a woman of twenty-seven with a run-down farm, a big run-down house, and all her energies and commitment invested in a business that made no sense without David; and David, if he lived, would likely be a cripple all his days. If he couldn't ride, I didn't see how they could keep Foxford, so Ellen was going to lose her home as well.

The door opened again, and this time it was news. Grace Markham had been the surgeon: that was good news in itself. She had come straight from theatre, pausing only to shed her gown and gloves.

"The operation went very well," she told Ellen. "The bullet's out, and he seems to be responding well. I think he's out of danger. He's a strong, fit young man; you'll be surprised how quickly he starts recovering.

"What we can't know yet," she went on in the same careful tone, steering a cautious way round the shoals of premature optimism and undue despair, "is exactly how much damage has been done. The spine is affected, but the spinal cord appears to be intact. I think we have to expect an initial paralysis below the waist, but I'm hopeful it will be only temporary. It could last a matter of days or a few weeks; it could last months and still right itself eventually; or there could be some permanent loss of function.

"I'm sorry I can't be more definite. We've learned a lot about treating spinal injuries, but we still find it very difficult to make an accurate early prognosis. All I can tell you is that I've seen people with worse injuries walk out of my office, and one ran."

It was about all she could say. The fact that doctors are gradually accepting that patients and their families have a right to be told what's happening to them is good but no answer to the fact that sometimes doctors don't know. She had told us the best and the worst. Only time would supply the truth.

Ellen said, "Can I see him?" Her voice was full of tears, but for the moment I think all she knew or cared about was that she still had a husband, not a funeral to arrange.

Grace smiled. She looked tired. I doubt if there are many occupations more physically, mentally, and emotionally draining than surgery. "Just a peep. He won't know you're there, not yet; come back in the morning when he's feeling a bit more human."

I gave her five minutes, then went to post-op to collect her. She was standing in the corridor, watching through a glass screen. I don't know what she could see: all I could see was a confab of monitors chattering over a vaguely human shape under a blanket. If I hadn't known, I don't think I'd have recognised it as David.

That hit harder than I expected. I'd seen a lot of vaguely human shapes under blankets in my time, and quite a few under shrouds, and mostly I had seen them in terms of treatment proceeding or failed. This wasn't the first time I had seen a friend in this position either, but it was still revealing how very different it felt to be personally rather than professionally involved. It was a reminder, and a reminder was sometimes necessary that all those vaguely human shapes that held a professional interest for people like me represented a personal disaster to their families and friends. Alienation is something doctors have to fight against, even ex-doctors.

I had told Sergeant Ross that I would take care of Ellen. When I had her installed in the car, I asked where she wanted to go.

She thought abstractedly for a moment. "Home?" It was more a question than a decision.

I started the engine. "Yes, I think we should go there first. Harry will want to know how David is, and how you are. He may have some questions for us too. After that, you have three choices. You can stay at Foxford, though from experience I suspect you'll have the patter of size-11's round the place most of the night. I can drive you over to your mother's. Or you're very welcome to come to us for the night. Harry's going to be tied up till tomorrow, so I'd be glad of the company. But it's just up to you, what you feel like doing."

She thought for a minute. Covertly I watched her face. Already she was getting some sense of balance about what had happened, a perspective. What had happened was profoundly shocking—to me, and so inevitably much more to her—perhaps particularly because of the utter pointlessness of it. No one gets shot for a Victorian hunting print and the sort of money David would have had in his cash-box. But already Ellen was finding ways of dealing with it. Perhaps she was facing the future; perhaps she was postponing that until she knew more of what the future held. Whatever, she was back in control.

I had known her a little over a year. I had valued her friendship, enjoyed her warmth, her spontaneity, her pragmatic sense of humour. I had known that under the well-scrubbed good looks, like a cover girl for *Horse & Hound,* she was a sensible woman. I had not until now realised how strong a woman she was. In the split second of a bullet's flight her life had changed. Perhaps she didn't yet know how radically. But she'd cope with it. Ellen Aston might be down, but she sure as hell wasn't out.

"No, I want to be home," she said. She managed a smile. "I'll put up with the Harry Marsh Formation Clumpers. I'll phone Ma from there, let her know what's happening. Clio, can I push your kindness a bit further? Will you stay over? Just tonight. I don't want to have breakfast alone tomorrow."

I squeezed her hand, glad to be able to help. "Of course I'll stay. Can I have the four-poster?"

"If you don't mind sharing it with twelve generations of wood-worm."

We were back at Foxford just after midnight. The place was lit up like a Christmas tree; there seemed to be a light burning in every room. Policemen were distributed almost as liberally.

I left Ellen in the drawing-room calling her mother, and went to look for Harry in the study. I didn't want Ellen following me in there. Scenes of crime tend to be bloody, and even more than the blood and the chalk marks, the immediacy of the sorroundings, their very familiarity, is an unexpectedly forceful reminder of what has happened. I thought I was over the shock, but David's chair still on its side in front of the desk where he had fallen with an intruder's bullet in his back knocked the wind out of me all over again.

"Harry, we're back."

He looked round. Now he was working, he seemed to have got his second wind. The greyness had gone out of his face. "Clio? How's David?"

I made a helpless little shrug. I didn't really know how to answer. "He's alive. He seems to be out of danger."

"Good." Harry was watching me closely. He knew there was more.

"His spine's damaged. They can't say how badly. He may walk again. He may ride. But Harry, I don't think he'll ever ride competitively again."

I heard the catch in my voice and turned away. If there's one thing a Detective Superintendent needs less at the scene of a shooting than his own wife, it's his own wife blubbing on his sleeve. I'd spent the guts of two hours being strong for Ellen; now I needed someone to be strong for me. But it couldn't be Harry, or not here and now.

He made a moment for me though, his great bear's arm round my shoulders steering me back into the hall. "Come on, love. The main thing is he's going to be all right."

"All right? What does that mean?" I was tired, not far from

tears, and taking it out in anger. "He's alive. He's paralysed from the waist down. He may get some use in his legs, he may not, but he's never going to have the strength and sensitivity to do his job again.

"At ten o'clock last night he was in contention for a place on the British team at the World Three-Day Event Championships. After this, he may manage a morning's cub-hunting if the MFH takes things easy, but he's never again going to ride a class horse at speed over an international course. It's over. If he still has a career, it's going to be training other people to ride in competition. All right? Well, he isn't going to die of what's been done to him. But it isn't going to leave him much of a life either."

I had forgotten where I was, had let my voice rise in bitter stridency. They could probably have heard me in the attic. Ellen could certainly hear me in the drawing-room. She came out now, and if she was pale, she was also composed. She took my hand much as I had taken hers a couple of hours before.

"Clio, I know what this means. It probably means the end, near as damn it, of the life we've had. It's been wonderful, for both of us, but there are other lives; if we can't find one that suits us, we'll make one. We have our home and our farm; but even if we have to give them up, we'll still be all right. My husband is alive. You don't know him as well as you imagine, Clio, if you think that David in a wheelchair is going to be a cripple."

She made me ashamed. I couldn't look at her.

She patted my arm. "Harry, I'm just making some coffee. Have you time for a cup?"

The drawing-room was an oasis of calm. With the door shut you could almost forget the activity all around. The thick walls and the thick old windows kept it at bay. Forgetting the reason for it was harder.

Over his coffee Harry said, "What did you hear, Ellen?"

"Almost nothing," she said. Remembering filled her eyes and thickened her voice. "A noise—a crack?—and something falling. I thought he'd knocked something over; I didn't even go to see what. It was only when Clio was leaving, minutes later—" She couldn't go on.

There was no need to. Harry knew what had happened when I went to leave. He asked gently, "Did you hear the other noise?"

"Other noise?" She thought for a moment. "There *was* another noise, more from the yard than the house. Metallic—like a horse kicking an oil drum."

"Could it have been one of the horses?"

"I don't think so. They were all bedded down then, and there's nothing metallic in the stables for them to kick against."

"What else could it have been?"

She tried to think. Nothing came. "I'm sorry, Harry, I hardly noticed it. We were talking, I wasn't paying any heed to the yard. I didn't know it would matter."

"Of course not, how could you? Don't worry, you're doing fine. The next thing is going to be working out what's been stolen. When you've finished your coffee, I'd like you to come into the study and have a look round. He doesn't seem to have been anywhere else, though we'd better make sure. The cash-box is empty. The desk drawers have been forced and obviously rifled. Was there anything of value in the study?"

"Apart from my husband?" She said it with a smile. "Yes, but it wouldn't fit in the cash-box, even though £37 and change left a fair bit of space. Is the painting gone?"

Harry looked at me. "Clio said there used to be a picture in there. Well, it's gone now. Was it valuable?"

"I imagine so," said Ellen. "It was a Herring."

I blinked at her. "Pardon?" I could not, of course, hear the capital letter.

"John Frederick Herring," she explained. "You know, the racehorse man. He painted every Derby winner between 1827 and 1849, and every St. Leger winner from 1815 to 1846. Gilgamesh was a great Thoroughbred stallion of the 1850s; that painting was one of the last commissions Herring accepted. He died in 1865."

III

So that was it. David Aston had been put in the hospital and his career ended not by a real horse, full of pride and good living, trying to jump higher or further or faster than nature intended, which was something that they all risked, but by a horse of oils and canvas, under a dirty varnish, that had run its last race more than a century ago and then been immortalized for its doting owners.

I must have seen it a dozen times, chatting to David while he made up his entries and wrote cheques to his feed merchant or ambling after Ellen while she whizzed round with a duster, but I'd never really noticed it. Certainly I had never appreciated it. All that came to mind now was an overall impression of brownness: a brown horse in a brown landscape under a brown varnish in a brown frame. It hadn't looked valuable. It hadn't looked like anything much.

At least not to me, but then I was a Londoner until I married Harry; matters rural, and particularly equine, were a closed book to me. Soon after I met Ellen, she invited me to Badminton to watch David ride, and I'm sure it was all very impressive, but the only truly memorable part of the experience for me was the mud. You wouldn't believe how much mud there was. Several corgis disappeared in it and were never seen again.

"Was it insured?" asked Harry.

"Oh yes," said Ellen. "I don't know for how much, but it's on the inventory of effects that came to David with the house. I don't know how long it's been in the family, but I know David's grandfather had it. Is that what they came for, do you think?"

"They?"

"They, he—whoever. Is that why David was shot?"

"It rather looks that way, doesn't it?" I hadn't been married to Harry Marsh for fifteen months without knowing when he was hedging. "It's not the first burglary on The Brink this year. Stand-ings was turned over back in January."

"I hope you don't find it," Ellen spat with sudden venom. "I hope we never see it again. The insurance will be more use to us, and I don't think I could bear to see it hanging there again."

"The insurance," said Harry, a thoughtful echo. "If it's that valuable, were there any special conditions relating to it—alarms, sensors, that sort of thing?"

"David could tell you for sure," she said, and then stopped, wincing.

"I know he will," said Harry, that marvellously solid reassur-ance in his face and voice, "in just a day or two. But it would be helpful to have some idea now."

Ellen nodded and swallowed. "We had a security assessor here once. I don't recall exactly what he said, but he was pretty well satisfied. Both house and stables are tied into the alarm system; with valuable horses, half of them other people's, around the place we reckon to be careful. Foxford isn't Fort Knox, but we always reckoned we had enough security to scare off the casual thief and make the professional look for something easier."

There had been nothing casual about the man who stole David Aston's Herring. He had come prepared for any resistance he might meet, prepared, actually, to pre-empt any resistance. David had been shot in the back while seated at his desk, before he had the chance to turn and see the intruder. There was a cold-blooded-ness about that which was neither casual nor professional.

"But the alarm didn't go off."

Ellen shook her head. Her expression was faintly apologetic. "The alarm wasn't on. It was a warm evening; when I took Da-vid's coffee in, he had the French windows open. It's only a little room; it can get awfully stuffy."

The thief hadn't even had to break in. All he had to do to gain access to the painting was disable the man working beneath it.

Harry was nodding, as if that explained something which had bothered him. "I wondered why he'd come while it was still daylight. Burglars generally prefer the dark. He must have figured that on a warm evening there was a good chance of a door or window somewhere being left open and therefore the alarm not set." He was thinking aloud. The Cotswold in his accent was always at its most pronounced when he was thinking aloud.

Ellen was staring at him in fresh horror. "You mean it was someone who knows us—who knows our routine?"

"It's possible, but it doesn't necessarily follow. It could have been a lucky guess; you aren't the only household in the country where the last one to bed locks up and sets the alarm. Or he may have watched and seen David working in there with the French windows open once before. But yes, we should consider the possibility that it's someone you know, maybe someone who's been here while you've been locking up. Does that suggest anyone to you?"

Ellen considered for the briefest of moments and answered without hesitation. "You two and my mother."

There are those who will tell you that my husband has no sense of humour. They are mistaken. What he has is a rather solemn sense of humour. Deadpan, he said, "Apart from us."

She sighed. The weariness came back to envelop her. "Oh Harry, I don't know. I can't think. Of course we've had people here—owners and other riders mostly—but I don't know if any of them knows when we lock up, or cares. I'm sorry."

Harry stood up. "No, I'm sorry, Ellen—to keep you sitting here at one in the morning after the evening you've had. Are you up to a quick look round the study before you go to bed?"

We went together. I saw Ellen stiffen as the shock which had hit me earlier hit her, but then she walked purposefully into the centre of the room and stood looking round her. Fortunately David's wound had bled very little, though I still found his tumbled chair disturbing.

Ellen pointed at a brighter rectangle of wallpaper over the desk. "*Gilgamesh* was there. The cash-box was in the bottom drawer of the desk, although it wasn't up to shoeing more than two horses at a time. There was nothing at all in those other drawers—old schedules and programmes, paperwork for the VAT-man, cuttings he'd kept for one reason or another. Nothing of any value."

"What about the filing cabinet?'"

Ellen looked surprised. "There's nothing valuable in there. It's for storage, not security. We don't even lock it."

"Can you tell if it's been rifled?"

She opened it, ran her fingers over the folders rather vaguely. "It all looks pretty normal."

"That's what I thought," said Harry. "Which is a little strange. You'd be surprised how many valuables are kept in filing cabinets, even unlocked ones, but no thief would. It's one of the places a professional thief would always look. David was using it just before he was shot, but still the intruder didn't bother checking it, even though he hunted for the cash-box and broke that open." His broad face creased up. Another mistake people make about Harry is thinking he's thick. "It's odd, that."

I had followed his reasoning. I raised an eyebrow at him. "Amateur night?"

"Could be, I suppose." His eyes were travelling slowly round the cornice of the room, seeking inspiration. "Ellen, does David have any enemies? Do people in his line make the kind of enemies who would hurt someone like that and make it look like robbery to cover their tracks?"

The appalling idea sank visibly into Ellen's mind. "You mean someone came here to kill David?"

"Oh no." Harry was quite firm on that. "No. Whether or not it was a robbery, whoever shot him never intended him to die. There's powder-burn on his shirt, so he was shot at close range. The only bullet fired got him in the lower back. That's a long way from heart or head, and if it was just a bad shot, he'd have fired again.

"Also, it was a .240. A deer rifle. You can certainly kill with a .240, but it's not really an assassin's gun. For murder you can't beat a shotgun: they're everywhere in the countryside, lethal in comparatively inexpert hands, and it's a lot harder to pin a particular injury on a particular gun the way you can with a rifle. Can you think of anyone who might want to hurt David, short of killing him?"

Again Ellen answered without hesitation. "No. My husband has never made an enemy like that. I doubt if anyone in eventing has. It's not that sort of business. With everything against you, from the weather and the bank and the course-builders and the horses to plain old fate itself, a rider's only friends are other riders. It's not as if it was a race: each of them competes against the conditions, not the other entries. You don't make rivals that way, let alone enemies. I don't believe it."

And perhaps she was right. It was a world, a kind of life, she knew much better than I. What I knew of professional sport, of any sport above the college level, I had learned from newspapers and TV. But perhaps not being involved, watching from a distance, gave me a perspective she could not share. I could believe it. I could believe almost anything of sportsmen, except sportsmanship.

Long before dawn the four-poster in Ellen's guest-room stopped feeling historically romantic and started feeling lumpy. No wonder Queen Elizabeth I slept in so many: she was looking for one that gave her a decent night's rest.

The bed was the main reason I was up at six-thirty. Ellen had a stronger one. Finally alone in the sprawling house, we ate breakfast together in the kitchen, and then I helped her to feed the horses.

There were eight of them in the stables, more in the fields. David had a couple of girl grooms who came in on a daily basis to help with them, but they didn't arrive until eight and by then either the horses had been fed or the stable doors had been kicked off their hinges. So it was eight buckets of breakfast cereal and eight haynets, eight pairs of wickedly mobile ears laid back, and eight big, muscular rumps swinging our way, thirty-two ironclad hooves dancing an impatient tattoo on the brick floor.

"Don't mind Lucy, she's all talk," said Ellen, pushing past the snake-headed grey mare with the curled lip and the glittering eye. "But watch the big bay bastard at the end: he'll have you as soon as look at you."

She strode from box to box, the full bucket in each hand apparently no handicap, her fair hair tied back with a scarf. When the animals were fed, she washed her hands and face while I telephoned the hospital. Then we drove down there.

Grace Markham wasn't there, but her oppo was. The news was encouraging. David had recovered well from the surgery and had been moved to a single room in the main block. He had had a good night, waking briefly around six—"That's when the alarm clock goes at home," said Ellen—and again and more completely at eight. He was rallying well from the triple trauma of shooting, operation, and anaesthetic.

I hoped this evident satisfaction with the patient's progress wouldn't lead Ellen to expect too much. "He's going to be very groggy, you know. Disorientated. He won't really know what's happened to him yet. He'll be very glad to see you."

"He'll know it's me?"

"Oh yes."

There was a policeman posted in the corridor. I went with Ellen as far as the door. From there, I could see David's face, pale as the sheet over him. They had a tube up his nose and another dripping into a vein in the back of his hand. His eyes were half-closed. Lying there, big and awkward and desperately still in the white bed, he looked very young and very vulnerable. I wondered if this was what the man who shot him had intended, or if he thought that a slug of whisky, a quick wiggle with a penknife, and a square of sticking-plaster would fix him up as good as new, as in the movies. Or if he had intended to kill him.

I stayed just long enough to watch his white face light up at the sight of Ellen; then I left them alone and went to talk to the houseman. "Any indications yet on the paralysis?"

He looked offended, as well he might. "Give the poor chap a bit

of time. He's still trying to work out which end of the sky fell on
him. Ask me again in a week, by then we may have some idea. Or
quite possibly we may not."

"Yes, I know." And I did; it was only that personal interest was
obscuring my professional judgement. If you can still lay claim to
a profession which you haven't practised for five years.

"He's a friend of yours, is he?"

"Yes. His wife was about the first person I met when I came to
live here. They live at Foxford, up on The Brink. Their land backs
onto our garden. David trains event horses. He was in line for the
World Championships team this autumn. I was up there when it
happened. We were celebrating." I became aware that I was bab-
bling and stopped.

"Autumn—four, five months?" The houseman sighed. "I can't
see it. Maybe the next one?"

"You don't believe that any more than I do."

"No," he agreed. "He may be lucky, he may make a good recovery. But it won't be the same as if it had never happened. Who did
it—who shot him?"

I shrugged. "A burglar. For £37 and a painting."

"Have the police picked him up?"

I returned the look he had bestowed on me. "Give the poor
chaps a bit of time. Ask me again in a week."

IV

It came of something of a surprise that the disaster we had been
coping with for some ten hours only became public knowledge
with the breakfast-time news on the local radio station. When we
returned to Foxford, we found three cars in the drive and a cross-
section of neighbours from all over The Brink clustering uncom-
fortably in shocked little knots, hoping they weren't intruding,
anxious to hear the latest on David, wondering if there was anything they could do to help.

Ellen was marvellous. She'd been considerably cheered by seeing and talking to David, even in the state he was in, and she accepted the intrusion of these awkward, well-meaning people in the spirit they intended it. She told them how David was and what the doctor had said, and promised that when she was sufficiently organised to know what help she needed, she would ask for it. Reassured on both counts, they left.

"Thank God for that," sighed Ellen, dropping into a chair in the kitchen. "I thought they'd come for their holidays."

"Sorry, Ellen, there's still us." It was Colonel Fane and, two steps behind, his daughter, Sally. They'd come from the yard, through the back door.

"Oh, you don't count," said Ellen, "you're practically family. Stay for coffee. In fact, if you wouldn't mind making it, I'd better tell the girls what's happening. Are they down the yard?"

"Actually," said Sally, "that's why we're here. Jane's mother came by to say Jane won't be back until matters are cleared up to her satisfaction. She managed to make it sound as if being shot in your own study is only marginally more respectable than having AIDS. Karen's on the yard; she says she can cope with the stables on her own but she won't have time to ride exercise and anyway there's a couple of those hooligans she wouldn't be safe on. So I thought, if it's all right with you and David, I'd come by and get them out for an hour apiece every day. At least until you can fix up something better."

Ellen was clearly touched. "Bless your heart, Sally! But you can't; there's eight of them."

"So I'll give them forty minutes each. It won't be for too long; you'll need to replace Jane, and then Karen can do the sensible ones and I'll do the loonies."

"And when will you do Pasha?"

"Over lunch, with a sandwich in one hand. Pasha's no problem; if he could drive the box, he could go eventing without me. Besides, he's nothing scheduled for three weeks; and besides that, he isn't going to the World Championships."

Ellen said quietly, "Do you suppose David is, now?"

Sally's dark head came up with a sharp determination that was almost tactile. She was a very determined person. She was Ellen's height and broader across the shoulders, and her hair was a mane of black curls tossing round a strong, almost pugnacious face. The laughter in her eyes was usually a saving grace; but she wasn't laughing now, and without it she looked like an Amazon.

Her voice was low, full, and rounded. "I don't know," she said. "You don't know. As I understand it, nobody knows that yet. But one thing is sure. If David can ride and if he's picked to ride, his horses are going to be fit for him to ride."

Ellen touched her hand. "Thank you. It'll be an enormous help, whatever happens. And I don't suppose we'll have all eight of them long. Half of them aren't ours; they'll probably go when I call the owners and tell them David won't be riding, at least for a while."

"That's true enough," grunted Sally. "Owners like you to be out there winning, they haven't much patience when you hit a problem."

Colonel Fane said, "I hoped I could help out with some of the office work. Let me call your owners and explain what's happened and how we're dealing with it. If they want to move the horses, I'll make the necessary arrangements, but they may not get in at a decent yard halfway through the season. They may prefer to leave them here and look for a free-lance jockey."

"You can tell them I'll ride any competitions they want me to," offered Sally. She grinned, a sudden impish gleam. "I haven't David's style or reputation, but I'm probably as good as most free lances. I've had a lot of practice getting second-class horses round first-class courses." Then she said, "What about Gilgamesh?"

That threw me. I thought, naturally enough, that she was referring to the Herring and wondered what she knew about it. My ears must have pricked perceptibly, because I found Ellen looking at me with amusement.

"The big bay bastard," she said. "David called him after the picture. The Colonel bred him and Sally broke him."

"He broke several bits of me too," Sally said ruefully. "But I rode him then and I can ride him now, and if David wants me to take him to a couple of events to keep him match-fit, I'd enjoy that."

Ellen said, "I'll be honest with you. I wouldn't get on him to save his life, and I wouldn't let Karen ride him. I know you can, and I'm grateful for the offer. But I've already got my husband in hospital; I don't want my friend there too. When his head's a bit clearer, I'll ask David. In the meantime, ride away at him—but please be careful. I'd sooner knack him now than risk him hurting you."

"I shall wear my crash-hat, back protector, and three soft cushions at all times," promised Sally.

Fane nodded approval. "Right. And then I thought I'd send one of my lads over to help out with the farm while you're up and down to the hospital."

The Colonel and his daughter had much in common and much that separated them widely. Both were tall and well made; his figure leaned to elegance, while hers favoured strength. He was an officer and a gentleman; she was not, would never have claimed to be, and probably had no wish to be, a lady. Both, from what I had heard, were capable of infinite hard work, and shared—with, it must be admitted, half Warwickshire—a passion for the horse in all its incarnations. The Colonel's primary interest was in breeding, with all the meticulous study and long-term planning that involved. Sally's was in the blood and thunder of competition.

They had a house on the far side of The Brink, behind Foxford Wood, another of these ancient little manor-houses, a pile of sun-bleached bricks with a Tudor heart all but lost in a maze of later additions, and very dubious plumbing. From all reports, however, there were fewer leaks in the roof at Standings, due not so much to the income from Sally's competition horses or even the Colonel's foals as the success of the farm.

The farm at Standings was the business which allowed the Fanes to indulge their hobbies. The farm at Foxford was David's stopgap for keeping body and soul together while he brought on his eventers. It was a difference in attitude which showed not only in the accounts but in the buildings and the land and the hedges and the stock. It was why the Colonel was offering Ellen a farm-labourer and why Ellen looked as taken aback as if he'd offered to lend her a stuffed moose. If David couldn't ride again, he was going to make a dreadful farmer.

Still, it was him and not Sally Fane who had been long-listed for the World Championships. Perhaps it was worth the price he and Ellen had paid, stepping round pans on the landing in wet weather and carrying water round the paddocks when it was cold because they couldn't afford the equipment to keep the field pipes from freezing.

Worth it, at least, up to last night, when everything he had worked and sacrificed for went up in a puff of cordite, leaving him with some first-class horses he couldn't ride and a third-class farm that needed money he hadn't got and labour he couldn't give.

Ellen said quietly, "I knew I could count on our friends for support. But I never expected this much kindness. I shall not forget it."

Harry came home for his lunch and to change the shirt he'd been wearing now for twenty-nine hours. Harry's shirts tend to look as if he's slept in them by the time he's straightened his tie in front of the mirror. This one looked as though he'd polished the car with it.

I'd made a stew. I'd made it in a pot the size of a bucket, and it would feed us for the next three days, regardless of what hours we kept and how long before we had to go out again. It was hot and filling; it even tasted quite good.

Even in his clean shirt Harry looked dog-tired. He hadn't been to bed at all last night and it showed. He'd only had his shoes off long enough for his feet to swell when John Martin called at our house on his way up to Foxford.

He'd have been better left to eat in peace, but I wanted to know. "Are you making any progress?"

He wrinkled his lip—at the question, I think, though it may have been the stew. "Yes and no. Yes, we're getting answers to some questions, like how many guns could have fired the shot and how many sports shops in the Midlands could have sold the ammunition. And I have a description of sorts. I went in to see David. He's still confused, of course, but he remembers being shot. And afterwards, when he was on the floor, he remembers the man stepping over him to take down the painting. But if you mean are we any nearer making an arrest, then no, I don't honestly think we are."

"But if you have a description—"

He gave me a jaundiced look. "Oh yes. Medium height, medium build, wearing a scarf over his face and a parka with the hood pulled up. I suppose that's all you saw too."

"Probably, though I couldn't be that precise about the detail," I admitted. "Could David tell you nothing about him that was distinctive?"

"Actually," said Harry, thinking about it, "yes. He was wearing a parka."

"So you said." I couldn't see that whittling the list of suspects down much. It would be harder to find a man of medium height and build who didn't own a parka.

Harry's gaze across the table was sharpening up. Behind the face like a square potato an agile brain was chewing over the facts like an intellectual garbage disposal unit. I knew that brain. It was dogged and determined, and capable of occasional feats of intuition, and I knew he'd been thinking about this on one level or another since he'd talked to David, aware that something he had said was out of synch and not aware until now what it was.

"On a night so warm that David had to open the French windows to talk on the telephone? Even cold-blooded criminals tend to work up a bit of a sweat: last night, wearing a parka with the hood up, waiting with a gun to shoot a man in the back in his own house, he must have been standing in a puddle. Why?"

To me it seemed obvious. "It was his disguise. Or rather—"

"No," he interrupted, a sort of grim triumph in his eyes, "you were right the first time. It was a disguise. The scarf prevented anyone seeing his face. The parka had another function: to disguise his outline."

"Face, outline—does it matter? He didn't want anyone to see anything they could pick out of a line-up later."

Harry looked down his nose at me. "Nobody is ID'd on the shape of their shoulders. You can say if someone couldn't be the man you saw, if he's too tall or too wide or too thin. But for a positive ID you need a face to recognise, and his face was already covered."

"So he was being careful. Belt and braces."

"Not if the risk of being noticed wearing a parka on a warm evening was greater than the risk of being recognised if he wore shirt-sleeves like everyone else."

That was true. A successful crime depends more often on passing unnoticed than on passing unseen. Ask any novelist. "You think there was something distinctive about him, about the shape of him, that a thick coat would mask? You think maybe he's a hunchback?" It was an attractive thought, but life isn't usually that easy.

"No harm in hoping, I suppose. But perhaps what our friend was trying to disguise was not so much his strangeness as his familiarity."

"You're back to the friends and neighbours who might know about the painting and guess about the open window and the alarm."

Harry nodded slowly. "I suppose I am." He works a bit the way the mills of God grind, slowly but exceeding fine. "Think about it. Suppose you're meeting someone off a train. If you don't know them too well, you look for their face and you're quite close before you spot them. But if it's someone you know, family or friends, you recognise the shape of them and the way they walk long before you can see their face."

Finally I caught up with him. "So the scarf would protect the thief from being ID'd by a stranger, but if David wasn't a stranger to him, he'd need the parka as well. A bulky coat on a hot night would also make him move differently."

"Very good," said Harry, and grinned. "I knew it was a good career move, marrying a writer of detective stories."

I don't write detective stories; I write murder mysteries—but it's a distinction which Harry, perhaps understandably, doesn't appreciate.

After lunch I kissed him, straightened his tie, and thought he'd gone. But a minute later his head popped round the kitchen door again. "And another thing. What was the metallic sound you heard in the yard, and why was our friend still arsing around the scene of the crime five minutes after committing it, with the police already on their way?"

He really did go then, without waiting for an answer. I don't think he expected an answer; he just wanted me to worry about it as well.

v

I didn't know what to do with myself. Incredibly, mixed up with the grief and tragedy was a sense of anticlimax. I had no place in this, no role. Fate had put me into the middle of it as if she'd had something in mind, but nothing I had seen, or heard, or done, justified my place in the dramatis personae. Even my skills as a doctor had not been required. I telephoned the police. That was a Second Grave-digger part if ever there was one.

I pottered round the garden for ten minutes, didn't do any weeding, didn't cut any grass, felt a growing urge to lop the tops off the snapdragons with the sweep of a bamboo cane, and decided to go for a walk instead. Inevitably my feet turned up the hill towards Foxford.

I had, of course, seen the man who shot my friend. But the brief sighting in the gathering dusk had been of so little help that it hardly seemed worth including in the plot at all. Even David, sprawled on his carpet with a hole in him, had seen more than I had—a height, a build, and scarf, and that improbable parka. I had seen nothing—a hurrying figure, possibly carrying a rifle, melting into the shadow of a hedge.

I hadn't even seen something that I should have seen. Unless it was about something nastier still, this was about a robbery, the theft of a valuable painting. Herring didn't work in miniature: you could spend a night under most of his canvases, hold a wedding reception under a few. The man I had seen had not been carrying *Gilgamesh,* at least not in its frame. You can always cut a canvas out and roll it up—though such treatment rarely enhances the value of an old and possibly flaky painting—in which case he might conceivably have stuffed it inside his parka. But if he had, why hadn't Harry found the frame? Nobody takes time and trouble hiding something they're not actually going to steal.

And what took him so long? A whizz round with a Stanley knife would have released *Gilgamesh* from its wood and plaster stall in about the time it takes to write it. Even on foot, the thief could have been well away from Foxford by the time we discovered David and the theft. Why on earth was he still there so long afterwards?

Walking slowly up The Brink, head down, almost unaware of my surroundings, I began to disentangle the entrails of two possible explanations. They were, of course, pure speculation; but if you know how a thing could have been done, you're well on the way to knowing how it was done.

If there had been not one thief but two, it might have been the job of the one with the gun to cover for the one with the painting while the latter removed that large and probably delicate item at a speed and in a manner consistent with its safety. It was the one with the gun I saw, the more mobile of the two, drawing any pursuit while his mate made unhindered for their vehicle. They must have had a vehicle waiting—a van or at least a hatchback, because you'd have trouble fitting that painting into an ordinary saloon, and however strange or ordinary their attire, they were bound to attract attention carrying a picture the size of a coffee table through the rural byways of The Brink as the sun set over Foxford Wood.

The other possibility was that *Gilgamesh* never left Foxford, was there even now, wrapped in tarpaulin and stuffed down a well or into a hayrick until such time as it was safe for the thief to return, under cover of darkness or some plausible pretext, to effect its removal and profitable disposal.

I liked that. It was how I'd have written it. It explained the delay before the thief made his get-away, and left him unencumbered to run off into the sunset, shed his parka and scarf, and face the prospect of a police roadblock with equanimity.

The rifle posed me a problem. With the painting hidden, it was the only evidence linking him to the crime; the sensible thing would have been for him to hide the rifle with the painting, severing that link and freeing him from any suspicion at least until he was ready to go back for them. He shouldn't have taken the gun away with him unless it could be traced to him, and nobody commits armed robbery with a weapon registered in his own name. Yet I had seen him running away, and by then, he had got rid of *Gilgamesh* but he still had the gun. Wasn't that what I'd seen?

The answer was, of course, that I couldn't be entirely certain of what I'd seen. I had taken it for a gun he was carrying, but I could have been mistaken. I was back in the role of Second Grave-digger.

But I would ask Harry how thoroughly they had searched the yard and environs. Obviously they would have searched—for evidence, for footprints, cigarette butts, or—since in Harry's words, you never know your luck—a carelessly dropped library ticket. They would have looked for signs of a waiting car, or the snag of wool on an overhanging branch hand-plucked from a particular Jacob's sheep and turned into just three Fair Isle pullovers sold on

South Ronaldsay in the summer in 1986. They would not necessarily have been looking for a hiding place capable of accommo-
dating something four feet long, three feet high, and just four
inches thick.

I was still trying, like a trainee juggler, to keep robber, gun, and
painting in the air when the clash of iron on the road too close
behind brought me jerking from my contemplation and diving for
the hedge. I will *never* understand the countryman's cavalier ac-
ceptance of roads without pavements.

The laughter which greeted this performance was not altogether
unkind, but not wholly sympathetic either. I looked up, nervous-
ness giving way to embarrassment, followed by the automatic re-
flex of anger, and Sally Fane was grinning down at me from the
top of a bright ginger horse hardly, if at all, smaller than St.
Paul's.

"Blackberrying?"

I cranked up a withering glare, gave it her full in the kneecap.
"Have you got a licence for that thing?"

"Are you coming in?" We were at the gates of Foxford. I'd
walked half a mile with my head down and my eyes turned on the
events of last night. By scrambling over our fuchsia hedge I could
have been here in half the time: the rolling English drunkard certainly made the roads on The Brink. "Ellen's away back to the
hospital, but I'd quite like to have a doctor handy when I get back
on the big bay bastard."

She was joking, mostly anyway, but I'd nothing better to do.
"Yes, sure. How long is it since you rode him?"

She thought back. "It must be four years. He's eight now, and
he was rising five before we sold him. He was that age before we
could have sold him to anyone but the meat man."

"Why?"

"He's a lunatic. He has all the ability in the world—never mind
going to the World Championships, he's good enough to win them
—but he's an absolute raving loony. I doubt there are half a dozen

riders in Europe who could have tapped into his talent the way David has. It'll be a real tragedy if they can't go."

I looked at her and shook my head. "David isn't going to be riding Pony Club games this autumn. Longer term than that, I just don't know."

We walked a way in silence, particularly when the crunch of my feet and Pasha's on the gravel drive was muffled by the occasional cushion of weeds. Then I said, "If David can't go, who'll go in his place?"

Sally looked sharply at me, then shrugged. "It doesn't really work like that. At this point there are still a lot more hopefuls than there are places. Some will weed themselves out over the next couple of months, with loss of form and soundness problems. The four team and two individual places won't be decided until after the final training session, so you really couldn't say who'll take whose place. There are too many variables."

That little whistle and crunch was a theory biting the dust.

Sally put her horse in an empty box and swung the tack off him. "Poor Pasha. The extent of his training over the next couple of weeks is going to be hacking over from Standings twice a day."

"How long does it take you?"

"Twenty minutes. The main reason I went home for my lunch was to give him another outing. It's a good job he's an old hand; you couldn't keep a young eventer ticking over on eighty minutes' roads and tracks a day."

"Roads and tracks? I'd have thought you'd come across country."

She shot me a sharp look. "You may not have noticed, but there's a damn great wood in the way."

"They don't let little things like that stop them at Badminton."

She grinned. She didn't have a great sense of humour, and it had taken until now for her to realise I was teasing her. "No. Well, they have certain advantages at Badminton. Like enough space to ride between the trees, and room under them for something bigger than a Shetland pony, and turf under foot instead of old snaggled roots and bedsteads, and to get into and out of Huntsman's Close, you jump properly made fences, not thirty years' accumulation of barbed wire, and—"

"There wouldn't be the same risk of tripping over a courting couple either."

Sally thought for a moment. "They'd make an interesting jump," she said then. "You could stick a red flag at the head end and a white flag at the feet end, and call it Lovers' Leap."

We chuckled, and the groom Karen led out Gilgamesh.

He was as high as a house. The afternoon sun glinted off a hide like polished bronze, a rich darkness with blood and mahogany in its depths. His mane and tail flowed like black silk and tossed like a wild night sea. Chiselled ears raked the sky. From their lofty vantage, eyes as cold and hard and brilliant as obsidian scanned imperiously across distances we could not comprehend. Limbs as strong and improbably slender as steel cables fell plumb-straight from great bunching muscles that played constantly under the skin and sent ripples of sunshine shimmering across his coat.

When the far distance ceased to occupy him, he turned the tapered head on its long flexible neck my way and condescended to give me a look. But it wasn't a look of recognition, or curiosity, or just plain interest. It has been called the look of eagles, but it was the sort of look an eagle only gives his lunch. A horse's nose is two feet long and an excellent thing for looking down.

I whispered, "Jesus," reverently.

"Jesus nothing," said Sally, "he thinks he's God. And I've got to get on him and tell him he's rushing his transitions."

Karen the groom, her eyes fixed firmly on the toes of her boots, murmured, "David says he gets further by asking him than by telling him." She'd been with David as long as I'd known him, and we'd nodded a greeting numerous times, but it was the first time I'd heard her speak. She was barely out of her teens.

Sally looked at her rather as the horse had looked at me. "Do you want to ride him?"

Karen looked up then. "Yes. But I'm not good enough." It was an honest answer, and it must have cost her something to give it, and I admired her for it.

"Well I am." Sally swung herself up into the saddle, wheeled the horse deliberately and trotted him up the alley to the top yard. After a moment, I followed her round the byre to the sand school.

I had expected—let's be honest here, I had hoped for—fireworks. Eventing is one of those sports, like motor-racing, skiing, and dinghy-sailing, where the chief interest for the spectator lies in things going wrong. All those people clustered knee-deep in mud round the lake at Badminton aren't jostling for the best possible view of people jumping it right. They've gathered like vultures for the prospect of distinguished and occasionally royal personages nosediving into two feet of cold water and pondweed. And it was in much the same spirit that I followed Sally Fane and the big bay bastard round to the school.

And I was disappointed, because (a) there aren't a lot of lakes in the average sand school and (b) they weren't jumping anyway. Mostly they were trotting: forwards, sideways, in straight lines, on circles, even on the spot. I could tell that she was doing different things with him within that one pace and that some of them he accepted and some he fought until his frustration flew in foam from his bit and high kicks from his silver heels; but still it lacked the sheer *élan* of people diving fully clothed into a lake and horses diving in after them.

I watched for ten or fifteen minutes, with admiration but also the same feelings I get watching acrobats: how do they do it—and why do they bother? Then I started back towards the house. I hadn't heard Ellen get back, but I thought I'd go and see. I walked back up the narrow concrete strip between the byre and the field. The big brick building was empty now, a silent echo of its winter self, when beef cattle filled it with low throaty music and the shuffle and press of bodies.

Thinking deeply unimportant thoughts like this and not looking where I was going, I tripped over the raised edge of a manhole cover, took three enormous strides like a trainee giant test-driving his seven-league boots, and then surrendered to the inexorable demands of gravity and sat down.

Nothing was hurt but my dignity. I got up and dusted myself off, intensely grateful that the cattle had been gone for a couple of months now, and glared at the iron cover as if it had ambushed me and leapt on me, wrestling me to the ground. I believe I swore at it and called its parentage into question.

While I was thus engaged, a shout behind me drew my attention, and I looked back just in time to see Sally and the big bay hurtle over the closed gate of the school. The horse's ears flattened evilly to his skull; he came belting towards me, filling the passage with the clatter of hooves and my heart with an unexpected, primitive fear.

My eyes could see that there was room, if not much, for the thundering animal to pass me by unharmed on his career up to the yard and that he was still approximately controlled by a competent rider who would not let him run me down. But my mind saw only an animal bigger and infinitely stronger than myself bearing down on me at a speed I could not match, and instinct bred in my forebears when they were just a race of naked apes, running scared of nearly everything that moved, surged up through the sophisticated patina of civilisation and sent me reeling against the byre wall, shrinking against it. I think if it had been less solid, I'd have tried to go through it.

My eyes averted, I didn't see the horse pass. But I heard the thunder of his hooves mount to a crescendo, felt his hot breath gusting on my cheek and hair, and smelled the hot, sweet, musty scent of hay and sweat; and then in a single climactic moment of terror it was gone.

I dug myself out of the me-shaped dent in the brick and hesitantly looked round. Sally was hauling the creature to a halt at the top of the yard, behind the house. Immediately she jumped from his back and ran towards me, towing him behind her.

"Clio, are you all right? Jesus Christ, I lost him completely there! Are you all right? did he hit you?"

He hadn't. I shook my head weakly. "I'm all right. I've just aged ten years, that's all."

Sally bit her lip. Relief was threatening to make her chuckle. "God, I'm sorry, Clio. I never thought he'd take that gate. It can't be far off five feet." It wasn't: I'm five foot one and I couldn't see over it. "The sod! He *wouldn't* engage his back end; I booted him in the ribs, and before I knew it, we were airborne.

"All the same, it's not funny; he could have hurt you. And it was my fault, because if I can't control him better than that, I've no business being on him." Her brows gathered, a wholly unreassuring depth of concern in her eyes. "Clio, you're as white as a sheet. Go into the kitchen and make yourself some coffee. I'll have to take this hooligan back and make him do his job, but I'll be in a bit later. I'm really sorry we scared you like that."

The blood was flowing back up my legs. It reached my knees and stopped them bending both ways, forced its way past the knot of my stomach, and steadied the racing of my heart to a mere healthy jog. But instead of stopping there, it went on rising: a crimson tide surging up my throat and through my cheeks. I was mortified by my absurd over-reaction to a little passing drama, too embarrassed even to snarl. For a moment I had seen myself—timorous, shaking, a town-bred dwarf alienated amid the calm strength and robust physicality of rural life—through Sally Fane's eyes, and I was deeply humiliated. I understood and sympathised with her urge to giggle, and only wondered at the obvious concern which supplanted it. I wanted to pull a paper bag over my head and crawl away.

I mumbled, "Yes, OK; no, I'm fine, really. He didn't even touch me; it was just . . . a bit of a shock—" Or something equally wimpish. Oh God, I hate feeling small.

I turned away with what dignity I could muster, and heard with relief the receding tap of iron on concrete as Sally took the horse back to the school, and let myself in by the kitchen door with a profound gratitude for the cool stillness of the empty room, the quiet of the empty house. Slowly the burning in my cheeks died down.

But it was not until the coffee had restored my equilibrium and the calm of the old house had settled soothingly on my soul that my mind was set free to consider the fact that I now knew what had made the metallic clang Ellen and I heard after David was shot.

VI

I phoned Harry's office. Harry wasn't in, but he was expected back. I gave Ellen's number and left a message for him to call. Then I went back into the yard.

If Ellen had been at home, I'd have asked for her confirmation, but in my own mind I was already sure. I didn't know what it gave access to or whether the thief had shifted it deliberately or, like me, accidentally, but what I had heard was the manhole cover behind the byre. If I didn't yet know what, it was clear that an answer of some kind lay in whatever hole it covered. It was time I looked into it.

It wasn't actually a manhole. It was a hatch cover, a bit under a yard square, made of some light-coloured metal, with handgrips let into it. It was seated into a recessed frame, so that normally it would have lain flush with the concrete yard. But however it was last replaced, at a fractional angle perhaps or with a bit of dirt between hatch and frame, it had not settled properly into place. One lip stood proud by half an inch or so. It was this which had tripped me.

I didn't know what was underneath—the water system, the septic tank, or maybe some esoteric service found only on farms. And I didn't know how deeply it was implicated in the robbery. It could have been standing up like that for weeks, and the thief, running with his arms full of painting, could have tripped there too.

But the noise I made, with the possible exception of the swearing, wouldn't have been audible from the house, and both Ellen and I had heard something quite clearly. To test whether it could have been the hatch being opened or closed, I bent to try and move it. Then I thought of fingerprints and straightened up. Then I thought of my handkerchief and bent again, wedging my fingers into the corner of the grip, where there would be nothing to disturb.

I didn't know whether I'd be able to lift it. But while it was heavy enough that I had to put my back into it, it didn't take my last ounce of strength. A small child couldn't have lifted it, but any adult could. I reared it back, and it settled comfortably against the byre wall with another melodious chime. It was, as near as I could tell, the sound I heard after I heard the shot.

Whatever it was for, it wasn't storing roses. A smell you could not only cut with a knife but spread on lightly toasted crumpets came up—not with great volcanic force to set me back on my heels but welling slowly and thickly like a great, heavy river. After a moment I stepped back to breathe.

There has been wide speculation as to what prompted Dante to write his *Inferno*. I reckon he stuck his head in a slurry tank.

My first impression—well no, my second impression, after the smell which was about as impressive as things come—was that it was dark down there. And so it was, but it wasn't black: there was light of a kind filtering through from somewhere other than the open hatch. There was enough light to make out a slick and viscid surface several feet below the grill still wedged across the hatchway. Adjusting, my eyes began to pick up a regular pattern of pale narrow bars in the darkness under the byre.

I knelt down, holding my breath, trying to see the source of this effect and understand what possible reason an art thief might have for opening his victim's slurry tank, and while I was thus engaged, someone hit me on the head.

The next thing I knew, a man's voice was saying, "She's coming round." But he was wrong.

I was still floating along quite happily on some personal high where the clouds were slick, brown, and viscid and the landscape reeling away below was barred with parallel belts of light and shade. Almost the only drawback to this life as a hot-air balloon was the presence of dragons skulking among the clouds, rushing out at intervals to blast me with breath like sewers out of their long, thin, horselike skulls. That and the band. I quite like a band when I'm in the mood, but this one was all thump and jangle, with about as much sense of music as a three-year-old with a tambourine. The drummer was good though. Great volume, great sense of rhythm.

Almost apologetically, bits of reality started pushing in. One of the dragons looked like Harry. One of the clouds was wallpapered to match Ellen's drawing-room. The drummer was still practising, though.

Harry said, "Clio?" Then, anxiously, "Are you sure she's all right? What about some more oxygen?"

The voice I didn't recognize said reassuringly, "She'll be fine. She just needs a minute longer to come out of it. She's been lucky enough."

Harry said, "If no one had found her—"

The doctor said, "The knock on the head wouldn't have killed her. But the gas could have."

I was near enough awake now that I could listen to what they were saying and follow the discussion intelligently enough, if rather remotely, without feeling any desire to join in or otherwise advertise my newly restored consciousness. I knew quite clearly what had happened to me. There were gaps, but they were in my emotional responses rather than my memory. I knew someone had tried to kill me, and how. Somehow I couldn't find any appropriate feelings about that. I thought I should be angry, and the fact that I wasn't rather worried me.

I said, "Who hit me?" and in view of the fact that I said it quite clearly, I was surprised and a little disturbed at how weak and frail it sounded.

Rather inaptly, I thought, Harry grinned. He sounded normal enough, so there was nothing wrong with my hearing. "Dear God, Clio, what were you doing with your head down a slurry pit?"

I explained. I explained about tripping over the hatch cover, and the sound it made, and when I'd heard it before, and about going to investigate what it was, and why a thief on the run with a gun and a painting should hang around for five minutes to play with it. And how, while I was on my hands and knees trying to see where the bars of light were coming from, someone hit me on the head.

I was sure I'd explained it right, so the glazed expressions of my husband and my medical attendant were both curious and irritating. I said again, "So who hit me?"

"No one hit you. The cover tipped forward and cracked you on the skull. If you'd moved the grill as well you'd have gone head first into the slurry. As it was, you fell across it; you must have been breathing the gasses for minutes. You were blue in the face when Sally found you. She gave you mouth-to-mouth."

"She called you?"

"She didn't have to; I was already on my way up here. I called Dr. Burke."

I was wrong. I did know the doctor—at least, I'd met him before. I sat up on the settee, sending the drummer into an ecstasy of percussion, and we exchanged a nod.

The door opened and Sally's head appeared. "How's she doing?" She saw me sitting more or less upright, and her face brightened. "You're back in the land of the living, then?"

"Thanks to you, I gather."

"My pleasure," she said, and grinned. "The least I could do after the fright I gave you. How are you feeling now?"

"I'll live." It was a bold and possibly optimistic assessment, based on very little evidence. "Sally, did you see anyone?"

"Just you."

"Someone hit me. I'm sure of it."

Burke treated me to his bedside manner. "It's not very likely, you know. And there's only the one bruise, and it corresponds to the hatch-cover Miss Fane lifted off you. You know what a knock on the head is like; it can give you some funny ideas."

I was feeling more myself by now. I began to bristle. "Indeed I do know what a knock on the head is like, Doctor. As a doctor, Doctor, I know knocks on the head from both inside and out, and it is my professional opinion that this one was not a knock but a blow."

Harry was getting that glazed look again. Burke put his stethoscope away, murmuring, "The doctor who treats herself has a fool for a patient and an idiot for a physician." The fact that he was right didn't of itself warm me towards him.

Perplexed, Sally said, "I didn't see anyone. I was coming up to the house to see how you were, and I found you lying on the grid over the slurry tank. Was there someone?"

I shrugged gracelessly. I couldn't prove it. I couldn't even say why I was so sure, but I was—I still was, in spite of the entirely reasonable explanation offered as an alternative. I had thought the hatch was secure, but I couldn't now swear that it was. It might have slipped. Nor could I claim to have seen, however fleetingly, or heard my assailant. It wasn't so much that my account lacked conviction as that I could offer no account.

But if you accept the witness of gut feeling, I had enough of that to sustain a theory twice as improbable. And the sequence of events did make a certain sense. The hatch-cover had drawn my attention by the sound it made and by being out of place, just slightly but enough to suggest interference. When I went to investigate, someone knocked me on the head, arranged the cover to make it look like an accident, and left me to suffocate in the poison gasses rising from the tank. If Sally hadn't been sufficiently worried about the fright she'd given me to come and check that I was all right, I'd be down at Skipley General now, on a tray in the freezer with a label attached to my big toe.

I tried to think. "There was light in that tank—not much but enough to see by. Where was that coming from?"

Harry favoured me with the patient, patronising smile of a man for his child or doddering parent. "From the byre, through the slats of the floor." He managed not to add, "Don't you know anything?" but it was there in his eyes.

"All right," I allowed, still not believing it but offering to meet him half-way, "maybe it was an accident. But ask Ellen when she gets home: that hatch is what we heard. It fits in somewhere. Somehow—I don't rightly know how, but I dare say you country folk can figure it out—you have to search that tank."

Harry's face was a study. But the fact that it came from me didn't blind him to the validity of the argument. Behind the horror in his eyes I could see his brain ticking over and his curiosity sharpening. Disgusting as the job might be, it was necessary to establish whether there was anything down there besides what the plumbing trade calls living daylights.

Dr. Burke wanted an autographed photograph of my head. I wanted to wait and see what was going to come out of the slurry tank. We compromised: I would wait and see what came out of the slurry tank, then pop down and pose for his radiographer.

Harry got on the phone and whistled up the world's largest vacuum cleaner. The whole business was very nearly quite easy but in actual practice quite difficult. The problem was not getting the slurry out of the tank: what goes in always has to come out eventually, and big vacuum pumps lift the stuff for use as fertiliser round the farm. Working the pumps may not compare with flower-selling for a job but beats doing it with a bucket and shovel by a long head. Our difficulty arose because we wanted to inspect what came out, an aberration the system designers had not foreseen.

They got round it by rigging a holding tank and pumping small quantities of slurry into that for a quick inspection before transferring it into the vehicle. It was a slow job, involving stopping and starting the pump and switching the hoses at regular intervals, and the stench that rose from the agitated slurry was such that no one could work in it. It required full breathing apparatus for the lucky souls poking through the holding tank with sticks, and those of us watching from the back of the house, forty yards away, stuffed handkerchiefs to our faces and got little relief. The drummer in my head made an interesting detour into Caribbean steel-band music, and I went into the kitchen and sat down, my eyes streaming, my mucous membranes on fire, convenient to the sink.

After a minute I had a stroke of genius and cut up an onion. If anything, my eyes streamed more, but the powerful antiseptic smell fought back the stench from the yard. Taking a deep lungful of the relatively uncontaminated air inside, I dashed out to press samples of my nostrum on Harry and the other observers. It didn't make their job pleasant, just—and only just—possible.

Sally stuck it out a few minutes longer, but then she came inside too. The stench clung to her like a veil. I cut up another onion.

"What do you think they're going to find?"

"I hope," I said, amending the verb deliberately, "they're going to find the painting, wrapped in plastic and waiting to be collected after the fuss has all died down. If they don't find the painting, or the gun, or a false moustache, or something you could call a clue, I'm going to be very unpopular in our house."

After quite a long pause Sally said doubtfully, "A false moustache?"

I grinned at her. "He didn't want to be recognised, did he? I reckon he was wearing the parka to disguise the fact he's a hunchback and a false moustache because he hasn't got a real one. Quasimodo did it."

She clearly wasn't very used to jokes, at least not mine. I don't think she was all that good on literature either. "I've heard of him."

I couldn't resist it. "Yeah, I thought his name might ring a bell."

It proved a longer job than I had expected. Ellen came home half-way through, amazed to find her yard full of cow-shit and her kitchen full of onions.

"What are they *doing?*"

I brought her up to date. She turned pale, even the delicate shade of green brought to her cheek by the slurry stench draining away. "You mean, he's been back here?"

I shrugged. "I think so. No one else does."

"But why?"

"If he did leave it here, maybe to pick up the painting. The police had gone, you were at the hospital, Sally and Karen were busy with the horses; maybe he thought it would be as clear a run as he was likely to get. He must have thrown a fit when he walked round the corner of the byre and found me peering into the slurry tank."

"Then he's been watching us?" There was an audible shudder in Ellen's voice.

But she was right. He'd done a lot of watching, from before this started. He knew the French window in the study was likely to be open on a warm evening and the alarm switched off. He knew where to find Foxford's one treasure. He knew where he could hide it and when he could come back for it unnoticed. He'd been very careful, very well prepared. He deserved better than me wandering onto the scene, uninvited and unexpected, throwing his plans into confusion.

I said, "I don't expect he'll still be hanging round, not after this. But if you'd rather not be alone, I can stay on up here for a few days. Or you can come down to us."

"I can't leave horses in the stables and no one on the premises," said Ellen; but she sounded as if she'd have liked to.

"Then suppose I move in," ventured Sally. "If you can put Pasha up too, it would actually be a fair bit easier for me than toing and froing between here and Standings."

It might have been true. Ellen didn't think so, but she recognised an act of kindness when she met one. She said only, "That would be tremendous, Sally, thank you," but it was clearly a considerable relief to her.

I said as an aside to Sally, "Let me give you a bit of advice. If she offers you the four-poster, take the settee."

Outside the pump stopped throbbing. The sudden silence was deafening.

"Does that mean they've found it?"

"Or that the tank's empty?"

I shrugged. "We'd better go and see. Anyone want a fresh onion?"

It meant that the tank was empty. Nothing except the obvious had come up the vacuum pipe, but when I thought about it, there had never been a chance that something the size of that painting would.

I looked sidelong at Harry. "I suppose now—"

"I know," he said forcibly, "I know. Someone's going to have to go in there. I've got it all organised, Clio. I've got a chap climbing into a scuba outfit right now. I've got a lifeline ready to haul him back if he gets into trouble. I've got a couple of men lifting slats in the byre to let in some more light. Is that all right. Is there anything I've missed?"

Mostly he was joking, though I'm not sure anyone but me knew it. I said meekly, "No, dear."

"I wonder how I ever made chief inspector before I had you," he glowered, a hint of humour in the depths of his scowl.

I patted his arm in a gracious gesture of wifely accord. "Oh, so do I, dear; so do I."

The man in the wet suit, possibly the world's least-becoming attire, tied the line round his middle, started his air supply and climbed down into the hole. We could hear him moving round in the semi-solid residue at the bottom of the tank. We could see the wash of his torch and the snaking of the lifeline through the hatch as it followed him around.

After perhaps a minute the line stopped moving and the torch went out, and a few moments after that the prehistoric head of a man in a wet suit and breathing apparatus emerged from the hatch. "I've found it."

It took them a minute to manoeuvre it out, but it was clearly what we were looking for. The shorter side of the frame was longer than the side of the opening, so they had to lift it up awkwardly on the diagonal. It was heavy too, with the big wooden frame and the accumulation of bovine waste.

Vindicated, I took my first deep breath for some time. It wasn't a good idea; I went back to my onion.

When it was lying flat, brown, and squelchy on the concrete and oozing down the hill, we stood round it in a ring and wondered what to do next. Was there any way of fingerprinting it?

Harry said, "We'd better unwrap it. We'll hose it off here, then take it down to the station."

The man in the wet suit, now without his breathing apparatus and dripping noxiously, said, "Something you should know before you turn the hose-pipe on it. It isn't wrapped in anything. How it came off the wall is how it went down the hole."

VII

Incredibly, he was right. That precious thing had been dumped in the slurry tank with no protection whatever from the filth and acids. No plastic cladding, no shroud of mackintosh, not even a sheet of brown paper tied up with string. He'd shot a man in the back to get it and then dumped it with no more concern for its safety than if it had been last Sunday's colour supplement. It didn't make any sense at all.

"I don't suppose," I ventured into the stunned silence, "that cow-shit is like peatbog and preserves anything that falls into it?"

I met a glum chorus of shaking heads. Well, I hadn't really thought so. "Then perhaps you had better hose it down—well, sponge it down—because anything under that lot that's still worth restoring is probably dissolving even as we look at it."

A man came up from Skipley Museum to co-ordinate the conservation of the painting with its treatment as forensic evidence. As he was arriving, with a box of tricks that made the average Scenes of Crime kit look like a make-up bag, I was leaving for the hospital.

I walked down to our house and drove from there. Driving your own skull down for its X-ray is not really sensible practice, not the sort of thing a doctor would sanction in anyone else, but I felt pretty well back to normal by then, and indeed, the X-ray showed nothing to worry about. The blow had only stunned me; the gas had put me out.

Before I got away, I was solemnly advised what possible symptoms would require further investigation, as if I didn't know my coccyx from my humerus, but the clear inference was, Don't call us, we'll call you. I went to enquire after David.

I thought he was sleeping and was about to back away when he opened his eyes, spotted me, and waved me over. The gesture was weak but deliberate enough: he not only wasn't at death's door but didn't even think he was.

It was now about twenty hours since he'd been shot. In that time he'd had an operation, a good night's sleep, and a couple of visitors. If it was far too soon to say that the rate of recovery had implications for its final extent, it was at least hopeful to see him harnessing his youth, strength, and fitness to his recovery instead of to frustrating it. Sportsmen can be terrible patients: they tend to expect immediate results and wallow in misery when they don't get them. A bit like doctors.

I pulled up a chair. "Hi there. How are you feeling?"

He grimaced. "Don't ask." The tubes that had hung round him like festoons last time I had seen him were gone now. His voice was breathy but unmistakably his own.

"Harry said he'd called by."

"Thank God he did. No one else in this dump was prepared to talk to me about what happened. They still won't talk about what happens next."

"They won't know yet. With spinal injuries it takes a bit of time before a picture starts to emerge."

"Then for God's sake, why don't they say that?"

"I don't know." Despite training and for twelve years practising as one, I have never really understood doctors. I have had some loud and vitriolic arguments in my time, and lost all of them, about the essential information the profession is reluctant to entrust to its patients. I finally decided that the guiding principle was not prescribing regimen for the good of our patients according to our ability and judgement (Hippocrates, born 460 B.C. approximately) but preventing anyone from finding out that we are only doctors, dependent on ability and judgement and then some luck, and not gods at all.

"How's Ellen managing?"

"Fine," I said. "Sally Fane's helping her with the horses; did she tell you?"

He nodded. "That's a weight off my mind. Sally knows what she's doing. She broke that big bay bastard of mine."

"So she said."

"She should never have sold him. He'd have come right for her, and then he'd have taken her anywhere she wanted to go. Still, selling youngsters is her business. You don't make much money keeping them all, and you don't make much more only selling the duff ones."

I told him about my close encounter with his star pupil, and he tried very hard not to grin. I got the impression it was the most cheering thing he'd heard all day. "And the police found your painting."

His head came up, his eyes rounding. "Where? Who had it? Did they—"

"No, they didn't get him. They still don't know who he is. The picture never left Foxford; he dumped it in the slurry tank."

David's face was a study in confusion. For a long time, although his lips moved, nothing came out of them but breath. Anger and anguish warred in his eyes. Then he blinked rapidly, and there were tears there too.

Almost from the moment it happened, when all his hopes and much of his future were ripped from him in the split-second agony of a bullet driving into his back, he had been struggling to come to terms with it, to find some kind of balance, some point of reference within the maelstrom of emotional response—the outrage, the grief, and the fear. And he had been getting somewhere, because greed was a motive that anyone could understand, even if it was barely conceivable that one man could have so much greed in him that he would destroy another man's life to assuage it.

And now I was telling him that it wasn't greed at all which had prompted someone to come to his house and shoot him down without a word while he was working at his desk with his back to the window. If there had been no intention to recover the painting, then the shooting was deliberate, personal, and incredibly vicious. How could he begin to come to terms with that?

But if there had been no intention to recover the painting, why had the man returned to Foxford? Could I have been wrong? Might my assailant have been no more than an imperfectly wedged manhole cover?

Finally David whispered, "Dumped? You mean, he didn't want *Gilgamesh?* He never wanted it? All he wanted was to do . . . this . . . to me?" Deep with horror, his eyes travelled down the shape of him in the bed, mapping that half of him under the sheet that only his eyes told him was still there, and then slowly up to my face. "Who hates me that much? In God's name, why?"

I took his hand and held it tight enough to hurt both of us, and part of me was a little embarrassed at this intense and intimate contact with a young man who not only wasn't my husband but was my friend Ellen's. But mostly what troubled me was a raging discontent that this sliver of human warmth was all the comfort I had to offer him.

In this hospital and others like it reposed such skill, such knowledge and wisdom and science, that its adepts could replace lungs and livers and kidneys and hearts, if not at will then at least when the will coexisted with the finance. And arguably more than that —they could create life where no life could have existed without them, in wombs which nature alone could not have filled. But if there was a gap in the nerve-chains linking this young man's limbs with his spinal cord, and it was no wider than that pin-head with all the angels dancing on it, they could do nothing to restore use or feeling or any life beyond the purely mechanical to those parts of his body beyond it.

And if there was no gap, they could look at the pictures their skill and science could make of it and say, "Well, he might walk again"; but they couldn't say when, and they couldn't say how well, and they couldn't even say whether for sure.

And me, with much of that same knowledge and wisdom supplemented by my own celebrated disdain for the sacred cows of medical theocracy, what could I offer him that was better, that promised more, that took greater cognizance of his innate human dignity? Only a handshake, that left both of us with bruised fingers and bloody palms. I knew no more than anyone else, not even why.

I found a voice, though it wasn't immediately recognisable as mine: people who thought me a cynic would have been surprised at the thickness of it. "David love, I don't know why. But if that is what happened, there is a reason; there must be."

He forced a snort of desperate laughter. "Clio, if you tell me it's all part of some cosmic plan, I shall hit you with a bedpan."

He'd known me for a year and still thought I had potential as a God-botherer? I shuddered. "I don't believe in cosmic plans, David, only human ones. Whoever shot you had something quite specific in mind. It may not have been theft—it begins to look it wasn't—but nor was it the random act of a passing maniac. Somebody stood to gain by putting you here and would have gained no more by killing you, because if he'd wanted to, he had every opportunity.

"I don't know who would stand to gain from disabling you or what the nature of the gain might be. But the nature of the wound is quite specific: it was always going to lay you up for a long time; it was never going to threaten your life. I don't think that was arbitrary. He had all the time he needed to make that shot and to make another if he wasn't satisfied with the first. He had time to steal a painting he didn't want, after all, and to dispose of it, all within earshot of people in the next room. That's not irrational behaviour; it's deeply calculating."

I was thinking on my feet, as it were, with only the vaguest idea of where the line was taking me, and maybe I shouldn't have been doing it in front of David who was weak and shocked and almost as vulnerable as it's possible for a man to be. Or perhaps he had as much right to know how the crime of which he was the victim was being investigated as he had to know how the condition of which he was the prisoner was being treated. Anyway, the argument was largely academic: I needed access to his thoughts in order to advance my own. Maybe that was pretty calculating too.

"And if it wasn't irrational, then there was a reason—a motive, a history, an essentially logical development from events in which you were involved. It's grudge or gain: either somebody's paying you back for something he blames you for or he's putting you on the sidelines because you'd have been in his way otherwise. Either way, this is personal.

"So there's no one in this world more likely to have the answers than you, David. You may have to go back years. You may have to rummage in an attic of cast-off memories for something so trivial you never gave it another thought. But it mattered to someone, because he's gone to a lot of trouble to set this up. Someone wanted something from you, and it may be your hurting or it may be something he couldn't have with you out and about. But it's the motive for this, and you know something about it, even if you're not aware of doing; and if we can isolate the motive, we can identify the man responsible."

He might be weak, shocked, and vulnerable, but David Aston was essentially a level-headed lad. When I finished the big sell, he said with interest, "Is this how you plot your books?"

Inside I flinched. If even good friends considered me exploitive, was I safe in assuming they were wrong?

I managed a grin, though it was a wry one. "Not really. I work from the solution back: it's easier that way. Also, the characters do what I tell them and don't go sneaking off on their own account when I'm not looking."

He smiled. Quite suddenly he looked tired; I knew I'd have to go soon. I patted his arm. "Listen, don't worry about it. Harry will sort it out; it's what he's paid for. You concentrate on getting better."

"Or what? Will you write me out if I can't walk again within three chapters?"

"No, I thought I'd put you in a stage play entitled *Whose Horse Is It Anyway?*"

He chuckled at that. As I stood up he said, "If you're talking to Sally, tell her thanks for her offer, and yes, if she can keep the big bay bastard fit, he might get to the World Championships yet."

He caught the pain I couldn't keep out of my eyes and smiled quite gently. "It's all right, Clio. I don't think I'm going to be riding him. But I'm going to make him available if the selectors want to put someone else on him. He's good enough, and there's time to do it, and he should have his chance while he's at the peak of his ability. Four years is a lot of miles under a horse; even if I'm fit for the next one, maybe he won't be. If they want him, they can have him. And if Sally wants to compete with him until they decide, his entries are in the office diary. She'll know who to contact. Just tell her not to get herself hurt."

I thought Sally would want to hear that right away, so I drove back to Foxford. The police had left; the smell had largely abated. Ellen and Karen were doing the evening meals. Sally's horse was in a spare box, but Sally herself was missing.

"She went home to collect some clothes," said Ellen. "She has things to arrange; she'll hardly be back before bedtime. Was it important?"

I rocked a hand. "She might think so." I explained.

Ellen nodded and smiled. "You're right; she will consider that important. You could call her."

"No, I'll drive round. I'm on my way home now. I'll just go the scenic route."

But I had no idea, when I turned right out of the gate and along the top of The Brink, just how scenic a route it was.

I had been to Standings a couple of times, to a dinner party the Colonel gave soon after Harry and I were married and later to the parish fête, for which he lent his lawn. It was a mile or so beyond Foxford as the crow flies, maybe twice that as the lanes wander; but people who haven't used these little Warwickshire byways can't imagine just how much they do wander. Nor how narrow they are, nor how overhung with hawthorn and honeysuckle. Two cars pass by, each shrinking into the nearside hedge. Two tractors don't pass: one backs up to the nearest gateway.

Grim, grey Skipley, with its cloak of grit and perpetual slick of drizzle, was centuries away, but only minutes by car. Its grimy urban fingers reached out to the hospital at the foot of The Brink. For the moment, the ring road held its industrious sprawl in check, but if that defence was ever breached, it would be up this hill in two shakes of a lamb's tail. Then Foxford and Standings would be no more than bus-stops on the town service, and the cottage where Harry and I lived would very likely be a pub, with a fake water-wheel in the garden and the sign "Kosy Korner" in poker-work over the door.

I was born and bred in the town, but it wasn't a town like Skipley, and anyway a year in the country had made a kind of rural recidivist of me already. Any time now I'd be joining Save Our Sycamore societies and Who Needs Motorways groups.

Held up at intervals by a bread-van, a school bus, and an agricultural implement I couldn't identify. A year in the country isn't long enough to come to terms with the deeper intricacies of the Massey Ferguson range; I probably took longer driving from Foxford to Standings than it took Sally to ride it. Finally I turned in between high brick gateposts and up the wide gravel drive to the big house. I think it was the fastest I'd travelled on that journey.

The housekeeper called Sally down, and I told her what David had said. Her face began to shine, with a strange dark glow that had a touch of fanaticism in it.

"Bless him," she said, and it was no mere figure of speech but an expression of religious fervour. "That's absolutely typical of the guy: the day after he's put in the hospital with a bullet in his back and no idea if he'll ride again, he's making plans so the horse won't lose his chance and the team won't lose the horse."

"Will they find someone who can ride him? You said yourself, not half a dozen riders in Europe could have got him to where he is today."

"It's a lot easier riding a trained horse than training him. Even so, this sport's full of perfectly good riders who wouldn't throw a leg across that saddle, even for a shot at the World Championships." She grinned at me then, a sudden ferocious gleam. "Besides, they may not get the chance. I'm going to ride him at Bramham at the end of the month. I'll give the selectors something to look at. If we do good, they're not going to throw me off the horse and put somebody else on."

Carefully expressionless, I thought about it. Perhaps I shouldn't have been surprised, let alone shocked. David wanted someone to ride Gilgamesh in the championships—why not Sally, who raised and broke him, who at least knew what problems the big horse presented? Clearly she was a good rider. Better than that, according to Ellen: only bad luck had kept her from breaking into the top rank along with David Aston and the select band of other event riders whose names the public know. She had the talent; she obviously had the drive. If she had David's horse she could probably go to the World Championships with as much chance as anyone else there. Maybe it was no more than fate reversing the swing of the pendulum, giving her the opportunity to benefit from David's misfortune as others had no doubt benefitted from hers.

Yet a tiny distaste stirred in me. It may have been more sentimental than rational, but I didn't like seeing her step so readily into the shoes of a man who'd had the legs blown from under him. There was something greedy about it. But I wished her luck and said I'd follow her progress with interest.

I went home then and spent the rest of the evening watching

bad TV with half an eye and wondering if, as we walked together up the drive to Foxford, I should have asked her a different question. And whether she'd have answered me if I had.

VIII

By the time Harry got home, he was fit to drop, and I felt like a worm for keeping him from the bed he deserved and needed. But I needed to talk about the spectre my mind had conjured up to haunt me. At least, I hoped and believed it was a spectre, a thing of horror but no substance manufactured out of coincidence by a deeply suspicious, if not actually unhinged, mind. What I wanted Harry to do was debunk my malicious little thought before it got ideas above its station and became a theory.

I said, "We keep talking about 'him.' 'He' shot David and 'he' stole the painting, and who was 'he' and where did 'he' go then? Is there a reason for that, or is it just habit?"

Harry looked at me as if I'd offered him a hamster sandwich. "What?"

"Have you some reason to suppose the crime was committed by a man?"

"Have you a reason to suppose it was committed by a woman?" It might have been a parrot's response, but it wasn't; it was a serious and astute question, and from that familiar sharpness in the tired depths of his eyes, he was looking for an answer.

Well, I wouldn't have raised the subject if I hadn't wanted to talk about it. I might have been happier asking the questions and ruminating over the answers for a while, but I wasn't blind to Harry's right, and duty, to require whatever cards I thought I held to be shown face up.

" 'Reason' is too big a word. But wouldn't it explain some things—well, one thing anyway? The parka. Covering her face would be a poor disguise if the rest of her body from her neck to her knees was giving her away. A sweater or a light jacket wouldn't do: it had to be something long and bulky. A parka."

Harry said, "Who?"

Even now his directness takes me by surprise sometimes, throws me off balance. "What?"

"No, who—who do you suspect? Come on, Clio," he said, in that special tone that senior policemen keep for junior policemen who put their own fingerprints on evidence and fail to appreciate the significance of back wounds in supposed suicides, "that wasn't a hypothetical question. You have someone in mind. Not Ellen, surely?"

"Good God, no." The very idea was absurd, not only because I had been with her when the shooting occurred. "Certainly not Ellen. Listen, I don't want to accuse anyone; I don't have any evidence. But—"

"But?"

"Harry, I'd love you to be able to tell me it couldn't have been Sally Fane."

I'd succeeded in surprising him. For a moment he said nothing. I could see him consider it, hear the rumble of machinery as his brain milled it through. Then he said, with no particular inflexion, "What makes you think Sally shot David?"

I shrugged, unhappy and defensive. "I'm not sure I do think that. It's just that—well, the idea occurred to me and I couldn't seem to shake it off. And it does have its attractions."

"Such as?"

"Such as the parka. Such as the fact that she was around when I was hit. And before that, when I tripped over the hatch, she damned near ran me down with the horse. If she wanted to distract my attention from where she'd put the painting, it was as good a way as any."

"It's a wonder, then, that she didn't do a better job of shutting you up," he said with a heavy humour that did not disguise the serious thought he was giving it. "What are you asking me to believe—that when she saw you go back to the tank, she hit you, stuck your head in the hole, and dropped the cover onto you, and then lifted the cover, pulled you out again and gave you artificial respiration?"

I started to bridle. I knew his doubt was professional and neces-sary, but I couldn't help taking it personally. "Yes, about that. You were already on your way to Foxford then; perhaps she heard your car. Or maybe she thought Karen was coming. Pulling me out might have seemed the only way to stop anyone wondering if she'd pushed me in."

"You're serious about this, aren't you?" Harry said quietly. "I mean, it's more than just idle conjecture. You think Sally Fane did it."

"I told you, I've no evidence. For all I know, she may have a watertight alibi putting her somewhere else for an hour either side of ten o'clock. I hope to God she has. But if you want to know what I think, I think it was her."

"In God's name, why?"

All things considered, he'd taken it quite well. He hadn't laughed in my face. He hadn't told me to stick to make-believe and leave the detection of real crime to those qualified to do it. He had listened and considered, and treated my fears with respect. And all that was about to end.

"I think she wants to ride his horse."

I watched expressions fleet across his face like cloud shadow chasing over a hillside. For a moment there was disgust, as if I'd played a shabby trick on him; then bewilderment as he wondered if he'd understood what I was saying; then impatience going on anger because, just briefly, he thought I was wantonly crossing the demarcation line between my world of imaginary evils and his of the real thing.

David had thought something similar. When I got my head clear of this thing, I was going to have to worry why people I cared about thought, even briefly, that I saw them as novel-fodder.

Finally Harry's features settled in a kind of wary, almost reluc-tant receptiveness, his credulity strained but not severed. He knew really that I wouldn't joke about this. He was ready to listen to an explanation of my extraordinary claim and to jump right down my throat if it wasn't good enough.

"You think Sally Fane shot David Aston because she wanted a ride on his horse?"

It was like facing the third degree. I had to keep reminding myself that I hadn't done anything wrong. I swallowed, took a deep breath, and tried to justify myself.

"David was on the long list for the British team going to the World Three-Day Event Championships. Not necessarily because he's one of the top dozen riders in the country, although he may be, but because he has one of the very best horses, Gilgamesh— he's called after that painting. By all accounts, he's a mad, bad, evil bastard, but he has more sheer ability than any other horse in the country, possibly in the world. He's not just *a* horse as far as these people are concerned: he's *the* horse, and whoever can ride him probably gets a ticket to the event that's the Leeds Piano Prize, the Royal Variety Show, the Bolshoi Ballet, and the Olympic pentathlon all rolled into one.

"Colonel Fane bred him, and Sally broke him and started training him. Then they sold him to David. I don't know the full story; from what David said, she was having trouble with him, but he reckoned she'd have got his measure, given time. If she'd kept him, it would be her facing selection, not David—and I don't think David would be in the hospital."

I was getting my hearing, and without interruptions. My pulse steadied, and I concentrated less on how I was saying this and more on what I was saying. "Maybe she thinks she still has some rights in the horse. Or maybe she doesn't give a damn so long as she gets what she wants. Every day of the week sportsmen and women do things and take things that will wreck their own brains and bodies, just for a shot at the big one—the cup, the medal, the title, the belt. If they're prepared to do that to themselves, is it so improbable that some of them—maybe only a few of them, but one or two—are prepared to do harm to their opponents?

"Eventing is a high-risk sport anyway. Any day David could

have ridden out to exercise and come back in an ambulance or a black plastic bag. She left it this late hoping something like that would happen and given her the same opportunity without the risk. But it didn't, so she made sure that he wouldn't be available for selection but the horse would. She wasn't particularly vindictive: she didn't want to kill him or even maim him: she used a small-calibre gun and we may yet find she was careful enough to leave him with no permanent disability. He's out of the World Championships—with luck, that's all. She's riding Gilgamesh at Bramham at the end of the month, and David's already told the selectors to use the horse if they can find a rider. She's got her chance; it's up to her now."

I paused, more for breath than because I had finished, and risked a glance at Harry's face to see how I was faring. I won't say he was sold—he never looks entirely sold, even when the judge reaches for his black hanky—but he was following closely and the strained credulity had given way to an open mind, still laced perhaps with that professional doubt but clearly considering the idea on its merits, without prejudice for its innate outlandishness. It was the best I could have hoped for.

He said pensively, "So what actually happened last night?"

I thought for a moment, then began to speculate. "She drove over from Standings with the rifle, the parka, and the scarf in the boot. She parked somewhere not too obvious—maybe that little Lovers' Lane effort that runs up to Foxford Wood? From there she crossed into David's big field and walked along the hedge and waited somewhere she could watch the back windows. She was waiting to get David on his own.

"Me being there was a problem. She expected him to be working in the study as usual, and she needed the window open because to shoot with that degree of accuracy she had to get close without him hearing and turning to face her. If the phone hadn't gone, she'd have been in trouble. Maybe he'd have been safe, at least for another day.

"After she'd shot him, she took the painting—she'd know about it; David named the horse she sold him after it—to establish a motive. If a burglar shot him, no one would ask who stood to gain by disabling him. But having it put her in danger, so she dumped it at the first opportunity. It took longer than she expected though: the frame was nearly too big for the hole. She must have sweated blood getting rid of it, and more blood again if she heard me coming out of the house behind her. A minute earlier I'd have caught her struggling with it half-way through the hatch and she'd probably have shot me too. I think she did try to kill me when she realised I knew what that noise was. If she could have made a convincing accident of it, I wouldn't be here now."

There was a long quiet while neither of us spoke. Harry broke it. "Does she know you suspect her?"

I thought back. "I don't think so. Last time I saw her I hadn't worked any of this out."

"Then it'll keep till tomorrow. Come on, let's go to bed."

But he hadn't quite finished. After the light was out and I thought he was asleep, a mumble came up from under the quilt. I raised it an inch and murmured down the dark tunnel, "What was that, dear?"

The bed humped and heaved as he turned towards me. There was enough twilight penetrating the drawn curtains for me to see the rough shape of him, long and bulky under the bedclothes, and for a moment the terrible tidy stillness of David Aston under his came to trouble me.

Harry said, "Do you want to just happen to be there when I talk to her tomorrow?"

I shuddered and shook my head. "If I'm wrong about this, I'm going to find it hard enough to look her in the face again. At least it's your job to ask embarrassing questions. If she ever accuses me of putting you up to it, I shall lie in my teeth and say that a nasty suspicious husband is the cross I bear."

"Thanks heaps," he said grimly, and the bed erupted once more as he turned his back on me.

"Thanks heaps," he said, with heavier and more sardonic emphasis when he came in for his lunch the next day. He threw his jacket at the back of one chair and dropped into another with enough force to threaten the floorboards we shared with the dry rot. "I have rarely been made to feel such an utter pillock in pursuit of my duty, and never since my old chief retired and went to run a South African gold-mine."

"Sally?" I ventured into a lugubrious pause.

"Sally indeed," he said venomously. "Sally, who raced over from Standings with a Little Paramilitary kit in her car boot. Sally, who shot a friend in the back so she could have a ride on his horse. Sally, who stuffed the Herring down the hatch of the slurry tank and tried to do the same to you when she caught you peering into it. Sally, who was entertaining her father and four other people at a dinner party at Standings while you were knocking back David's home-brew, and was still entertaining them when David came out of surgery. Sally, who couldn't possibly have done what you said she'd done if she was James Hunt, James Bond, and Mrs. Beeton all rolled into one."

We were finishing up the stew. I wished I had something more placatory to offer him. I said quietly, "Whoops," and wondered if there was any ice-cream in the fridge.

Trying desperately to see the bright side, I added, "You know, it would have been pretty awful if it had been Sally. For David and Ellen, I mean—well, for all of us. The Brink's a small community to have that kind of thing happening within it. Much better if it was a stranger."

Harry looked up at me suspiciously. "But?"

I managed a reasonable simulacrum of injured innocence. "But nothing. If you tell me Sally couldn't have done it, obviously I accept that. You're the policeman. You're the one with all the training, the experience, and the facilities. All I have to work with is a kind of gut instinct for what's likely, for those things that could have happened but wouldn't have happened that way unless certain other things happened too. A sense of the probable, perhaps."

"And?" He was still looking at me, much as you look at a magician with three egg-cups when the evidence of your own eyes insists that the marble is under the middle one, and all your instincts warn you that it isn't.

"And," I said, thoughtfully and carefully, aware that I was putting myself beyond redemption, even by a baked Alaska, "it doesn't seem probable to me that all those dominoes would fall into line like that unless that was the way they were set up in the first place."

CHAPTER 2

Roads and Tracks

I

She had more sense than to come looking for me, but the next time I showed my face at Foxford, she pinned me to the wall with the force of her indignation. "Your Harry thinks I shot David!"

If there's one thing being a novelist equips you for, it's lying. I let a look of weary despair wash over my face. "Oh God, not you too?"

That threw her. She blinked rapidly, the dramatic dark eyes startled and confused. "What?"

I sighed. "They've got Scenes of Crime specialists, forensic scientists, fingerprint experts, even a mounted division. Why can't the police force train itself some Asking Questions Tactfully officers?"

She didn't know what I was talking about, but I'd succeeded in knocking all the impetus out of her attack. "Er—sorry?"

"Harry," I said by way of explanation. "He's managed to offend half the population of The Brink—who, it will not have escaped your notice, are our neighbours—by asking what they were doing on Tuesday night in his best canny, gruff policeman voice. It's not answering his questions that people resent; it's his 'You can't fool me, chummy, I've got a Black Maria outside' manner."

The time had come when she had to say something. Her mind must have been in turmoil, wondering if she'd over-reacted to a routine, if irritating, consequence of a crime in the locality and whether I had noticed if she had. Finally, wisely, she elected to play it straight.

She shrugged and grinned. "That's a relief. Hell, I thought he was for real."

"Oh, it was for real, all right," I said. "He really needs to know where everyone was and who can vouch for who else. Finding that picture threw everything at the fan: if it wasn't robbery, then it was personal, and that means someone David knows. Quite possibly someone we all know. Ellen and I ruled one another out, otherwise he'd have grilled us too. I suppose you and your father vouched for each other."

She started to relax. "Better than that actually. We had the Maudsleys and Jan and Bobby Parker round for dinner. Just as well really; if I'd been home alone, I'd have been rather uneasy, at least until . . ." She let the sentence peter out.

I finished it for her. "Until they get her."

Sally Fane jumped out of her rose-tan skin. "Her?"

"Her, him—whoever. It could have been a woman: it was a gunshot, after all, not manual strangulation." I said it quite negligently, without import.

"I thought you saw him."

"I saw someone. It could have been the Archbishop of Canterbury or Dame Edna Everage for all I can say. I suppose the odds favour it being a man, but not by all that much. Women have passions, too, and grudges, and ambitions."

And with that, I gave her a friendly nod and let myself into Ellen's kitchen, and left Sally on the mat wondering if I knew or if it was just so much coincidence. Which was how I meant to leave her. I went to find Ellen and ask after David.

The Maudsleys were old India hands who had retired to England fifteen years before and never quite come to terms with the servant problem. They had a single frustrated peacock called Nabob, whose shrieks of torment were heard just rarely enough to go on disturbing. Mr. Maudsley tended to refer to Mrs. Maudsley as "the mem." But they were a decent enough pair of old sticks, even if Mr. Maudsley once tried to buy a punkah in Woolworths and it was rumoured they still slept under mosquito nets. I was quite sure they'd want to sign the get-well card I'd bought for David. I wouldn't have bought it otherwise.

The other people I was sure would want to sign it were Jan Parker and her brother, Bobby. Jan was a financial executive with a PR firm in Coventry. Bobby was a professional cricketer and author of the most exquisite hand embroidery you ever saw. He did it on TV once, in the background while somebody interviewed Ian Botham in the foreground. He said it relaxed him and did great things for his grasp and co-ordination. Actually I think he just liked doing it. When I showed him the card, he grinned, fetched a needle and silk, and stitched out his signature. After that we talked.

And after that Harry and I had one of our all-time, all-star, all-seats-sold, standing-room-only rows, which sent the cat scuttling for cover and knocked thousands off property values on The Brink because of the noisy neighbours.

Harry began, "How dare you—" and went on to accuse me of obstructing police efforts, wasting police time, subverting the cause of justice and harassment, partly of Sally but mostly of him.

I began, "Who the hell do you think you are—" and went on to remind him of the rights of the citizen, the freedom of the individual, the dangers of the police state, and the fact that my taxes paid his salary. (Actually, of course, the vagaries of the British tax system meant that the tax on my income was paid by my husband, a satisfactory situation from my point of view but hardly in the spirit of the Equal Opportunities legislation. Also, to be honest, whichever of us paid, my taxes wouldn't have kept him in crumpled shirts.)

When in due course we got past the mindless yelling stage and down to what was actually worrying him, it was not so much that I might be completely wrong, upset people, and reflect badly on him, but that I might possibly be partially right and my enthusiastic but undisciplined questing might alert the culprit in time to evade methodical police enquiries.

Anger had already faded; now my sense of righteous indignation began to wax pale as well. I was undoubtedly in the right, the police are society's weapon for dealing with crime and not a closed-shop warrior élite with first claim on anything interesting, but it wasn't wholly as a police officer that Harry was reacting. Dear love him, the man was my husband and he was afraid I could get hurt. Since he wasn't going to put his anxiety into words, I did it for him.

From the look of genuine amazement on his face, it was clear that no such concern had troubled him. He shook his head, ponderous and patronising. "Clio, it's like this: there's no point putting in a highly trained, highly sensitive police dog after the scene has been trampled by an elephant."

He was not, however, so scornful of the elephant that he wasn't interested in what it had found out.

"She spilled coffee down her dress."

His expression didn't flicker; his voice remained flat. "Sally did?"

I nodded. "She had to go up and change."

"Well, she would," he said, "wouldn't she?"

"Bobby Parker reckons it took her half an hour."

He'd have died rather than admit it, but that snippet of information struck a chord with him. "Does he now?"

Admittedly, Mrs. Maudsley thought it was nearer twenty minutes and didn't find it surprising, since the full cup that up-ended itself down her front must have soaked not only her dress but everything underneath it; and after she'd stripped, washed, and dressed afresh, her make-up would need serious attention too. Mrs. Maudsley plainly thought twenty minutes the equivalent of a two under par.

But even at twenty minutes, it was just possible. If they were the right twenty minutes.

Harry said, "About what time was this?"

I tried not to gloat. " 'About' be damned; it was exactly five to ten. The Colonel, it seems, always watches the ten o'clock news, even when he's entertaining. It's a kind of ritual. So at five to ten they got up from the table to take their coffee into the sitting-room, where the TV is, and Sally caught her sleeve on the door handle and baptised herself with best-ground Colombian, none of your instant rubbish."

"And how do they know what time she got back?"

"It was between the interval and the weather. Mrs. Maudsley thought it was just after the interval; Bobby thinks it was just before the end. Jan Parker didn't notice her come in, and I don't think Mr. Maudsley missed her."

Harry frowned, groping for facts in his memory like a small boy delving for sweets in a fairground lucky dip. "Your call was logged at ten-ten. You reckoned David was shot maybe five minutes before that, and you saw the gunman running away three or four minutes later. She'd have had to get from Standings to David's French window in under ten minutes, and back in about the same or a little less."

"It's about three miles. Even at thirty miles an hour, you'd do it in six minutes."

He looked out from under his eyebrows at me. "You reckon?"

So we tried it. We tried it with his car, which was big and powerful, and mine, which was little and nippy. We tried it in full daylight, and we tried it again when dusk was blurring the corners and sending the neighbours to their beds. He even posted constables at strategic points to stop the traffic—two of them found no one to stop, the third caught only Jan Parker on her way home from a meeting and Miss Withinshaw taking her Sealyham for his constitutional—so that we could do it without fear for the consequences, as if our freedom depended on it.

The fastest I managed it was eight and a half minutes down the hill and nine up it. The fastest times Harry recorded were a shade under and over eight minutes. The bends kept him from encroaching much on my time, although he had three times the power at his disposal. Jackie Stewart might have shaved a bit more off, but he'd still have found it hard going if Mrs. Maudsley's twenty minutes was accurate.

"She had to change," said Harry, "at least out of the dress into trousers. Then she had to get to her car. Let's be generous and assume that she came up the hill in eight minutes. She's already at least eleven minutes away from the incident with the coffee, and even if David was ready to be shot the moment she reached Foxford, she's still behind schedule. The lane to the wood is about the closest she could park, and she wouldn't get through the hedge and come up the field in under a minute. It had to take her a minimum of twelve minutes from leaving her guests to arriving at David's window. That's a couple of minutes after you and Ellen heard the shot."

"A couple of minutes!" It was a tiny discrepancy, a leeway that would vanish entirely if we'd allowed just a few extra seconds at each juncture or if the dinner party had risen just two minutes earlier than estimated.

"But those timings are already shaved to the bone; you can't take even seconds off them. In all likelihood, the thing would actually take three or four minutes longer than that. Accept it, Clio. Unless you know of some way she could have done that journey in under six minutes, she didn't do it at all."

But suppose it wasn't Jackie Stewart we had to contend but Barry Sheen? "I'll tell you one thing we haven't tried," I said. "A motorbike."

"Oh God," Harry said wearily as the day ended.

But the next day we were up there again, with a two-wheel hotshot from Traffic Branch. He did it four times each way, hugging the hedges and scraping the verges with alternate kneecaps. The first time he got up the hill in eight minutes. The fourth time he did it in six minutes and nine seconds.

"Nine seconds, Harry!" I heard both triumph and desperation in my voice. "You're not going to tell me I'm wrong for the sake of nine seconds?"

He put his arm round my shoulders and walked me away, like a child that was getting over-excited. To put his arm round me like that he had to stoop slightly. "The nine seconds isn't really the point. Suppose he'd done it in six minutes flat. He would have proved it was possible. He would also have established, to my satisfaction, if not to yours, that only a motorcycle ace with every-thing in his favour could have done it. Maybe Sally Fane can ride a bike. Maybe she has a bike or access to one. But neither you nor I could have done what you're suggesting she did, and even young Parrott there on the Skipley Flier probably couldn't have done it. We'd be flying in the face of the evidence not to accept that what we've done here this morning and last night is virtually eliminate Sally Fane as a suspect."

I bit my lip. It or something tasted bitter. In my own mind I had been sure, but Harry was right: if it couldn't be done, then it wasn't done, and if it could only just be done, it probably wasn't done either.

I sighed. "I'm sorry, love. I thought I had the answer."

Harry's fond, forgiving squeeze almost lifted me off the ground. "It isn't always necessary to have the answer, just some questions you need answers to. It was worth the try." He grinned. "If noth-ing else, we've made young Parrott's day."

"What will you do now?"

He stuck out his lower lip and blew thoughtfully up his nose. "I suppose, having got this far, I'd better talk to Bobby Parker and the Maudsleys. If they actually got up from the table five minutes earlier, the thing becomes possible again. Otherwise, we do what we always do—plug away until something gives. If it wasn't Sally, it was someone else; just knowing that is a help. You may even be right about the horse, just wrong about the rider."

I shook my head, despondent. "No one else could be sure to gain by putting David out of action."

"Could Sally?"

"No," I conceded slowly. "But she was. She is."

"So maybe someone else thought the odds were good enough to be worth the gamble."

"No one else had the opportunity."

"Sally didn't have the opportunity," he reminded me pointedly. "So someone else must have."

"And who hit me on the head?"

"The hatch-cover slipped. It was always the most likely explanation."

"Things don't always happen the most likely way."

"No. But it's most likely that they do."

II

Bobby was quite sure about the time. They'd missed the start of the Colonel's news through mopping up after Sally.

And Miss Withinshaw, when asked, said that she always took Podgy for his walk at ten and had neither seen nor heard a vehicle in the lanes at that time. She was out for about a quarter of an hour. She conceded that she might not have noticed a car going quietly about its business, but she didn't believe she could have failed to hear anyone making the kind of row we had made up and down The Brink the previous evening.

Ellen dropped in on her way back from the hospital. Her face was radiant. "Someone stuck a pin in his toe and he felt it!"

"Ellen, that's great news." I sat her down, and we celebrated with a bottle of elderflower wine I had from David's last foray into vintnery. It was every bit as bad as the one we'd been drinking before he was shot.

"That's what the doctor said," she said, a little calmer now. "But I wondered if I was reading too much into it."

I shook my head firmly. "No. Short of him leaping out of bed and tap-dancing his way down to X-ray, it's simply the best sign you could hope for. It means the nerve-chains of the central nervous system are intact all the way from that toe to his brain, and if one kind of message, the pain of the pinprick, can get through, there's every reason to hope that full two-way communications will be restored. Hell, I can't give you a guarantee, but if it was my husband's toe that was complaining about being pricked, I'd hold off signing the cheque for the wheelchair."

We enthused a little more about David's progress; then I enquired if she had replaced the truant groom yet. An idea was already stirring at the back of my mind, languourous and unfocused, a bit like blue-green algae wondering whether this sex thing was worth pursuing. Without encouragement they and I would probably have given up.

I don't know what did it for the blue-green algae. For me, it was Ellen rolling her eyes skyward and mouthing imprecations she wouldn't dream of saying aloud. "You have no idea the difficulty getting reliable stable-hands. Trouble is, it looks like fun. It appeals to young girls who think they'll spend the day galloping in slow motion along one skyline after another. They can't imagine the sheer hard labour that goes into keeping competition horses fit and well. Or how difficult fit horses are: just because they haven't fallen off at the riding school for three weeks they think they could cope. But if I put the best of the ones I've seen this week on the easiest of our horses, I'd probably never see either of them again.

"And if you take away the riding, they don't want the work—except for one or two who look about twelve, clearly think looking after horses is the natural development from playing with dolls, and would be steamrollered the first time they got between Lucy and her dinner. I don't know what I'm going to do. Without Sally we couldn't manage at all, but even with her we're barely scraping by. It's not fair to Karen, and it's not fair to the owners to skimp on their horses the way we're having to. The first attack of azoturia and I'm going to have a very displeased client and probably some empty stables."

I said, blinking, "Azo—"

"Azoturia," she said, and grimaced. "It's a cramping attack which occurs when fit horses miss exercise. It's a dead giveaway that you're not giving them enough work."

"Listen," I said. "I know nothing about horses. But I'm not twelve, I never liked dolls, I don't want to ride, and anything that tries to walk over me will lose its front teeth. I can't offer you any expertise, but I can offer you a few hours' labour every day to tide you over until you get someone better. I mean, how difficult can shovelling horse-shit be? If I take some of the load off Karen and she takes some of the load off Sally, that'll leave her a bit more time to prepare Gillyflower for Brand's Hatch. Yes?"

"Are you serious?"

And of course I was, because I liked Ellen and wanted to help her out and because, whatever happened to David's business in the future, I didn't want to think it might have survived if I'd weighed in with a bit of time and effort when it mattered. And because with a reason to be working round Sally Fane day and daily I might find out how it was she'd done the seemingly impossible. "Absolutely."

"What will Harry say?"

Harry would do his nut. "He won't mind. I can do a part-time job and still function as a wife."

"He won't mind you developing muscles like a navvy and smelling like a drayman?"

Passionately. "I don't expect so."

"One of these days," said Ellen, "when David's home and things are getting back to normal, I'm going to take time to thank all the people who've seen us through this, and you and Sally and Karen are going to be pretty high up the list." Well, one out of three ain't bad. "In the meantime, all I can say is, yes, it would be an enormous help, and yes, I'll keep looking for someone to do it on a permanent basis; and for God's sake don't forget you have other things to do besides helping me. Even an hour each day would take the pressure off; two hours would be a God-send. Mornings are the worst, if you could manage that."

I saw her out to her car. "By the way," she added, "it's Gilgamesh or The Big Bay Bastard. He doesn't answer to Gillyflower.

And the event is Bramham. Brand's Hatch is for sissies: it's all on one level and there aren't any jumps."

From her face and from her manner it was clear that Sally no longer believed my bland explanation of Harry's interest in her. She knew now that it was personal, that the police were checking up on her activities in greater detail than they were for any other resident of The Brink; by now news of Harry's official enquiries of the Parkers and the Maudsleys (as distinct from my amateur but perhaps more tactful probings) must have reached her. I couldn't tell if she held me responsible, or if it was just the backwash of her resentment towards the police, and Harry in particular, I was picking up. But there was something in the air between us, something unstated but sharp and electric, and I knew she was watching me as closely as I was watching her. I wouldn't be venturing too near the slurry tank again or any horse she was riding, unless there were a whole lot of other people around at the time.

I had made Ellen my offer in the full awareness that the work would be hard and probably unpleasant, but thinking there was a natural limit to how much hardship and unpleasantness could be crammed into any one morning. I suppose I was right, but I had seriously underestimated where that limit lay.

Have you any idea how much horse-shit weighs? How much it smells? How it rolls off the shovel and hides under the wheelbarrow the moment your concentration slips? Or how, when the last ill-favoured particle has been safely consigned to a muck-heap an inconvenient distance from the stables, the author of it catches your eye over his half-door, gives you a smug smile and lifts his tail again? King Augeas of Elis knew what he was about when he set Hercules to muck out his stables. Hercules had a bright idea, too, diverting the river Alpheus to do the job for him. I'd have given it a try, but the only river handy was the sweat streaming from my brow and it wasn't quite enough. Nearly, but not quite.

Nothing happened on the first day, except that I nearly died of coronary insufficiency five separate times. That evening Harry and

I argued again, but the argument was already assuming the outline of a ritual, observed more from duty than devotion. He didn't want me having anything to do with Foxford until the mystery was resolved, but he knew he was on a losing wicket. I wanted to find out if Sally was involved. Let's be honest here: I wanted to prove that I was right; bringing David's assailant to book actually figured a little lower on my list of priorities, though I wouldn't have admitted that then, but after a morning shovelling muck my missionary zeal was at a fairly low ebb. I would finish what I'd started, but I was no longer convinced anything was going to come of it.

So our argument was less vehement than the previous one. We had the TV on and we were arguing mostly in the adverts. You can't call that passionate.

The next morning I saw him off to work, then pulled on my wellies and climbed the hill to Foxford. And a little before eleven-thirty, while she was working Lucy over the cross-country jumps in the big field below the wood, somebody took a pot-shot at Sally.

The first thing we knew was a clatter of hooves in the yard and the grey mare shoved me aside to get into her box. Karen, who had been saddling Gilgamesh for Sally's next ride, slammed his door and came up the yard at a run. She cast a quick look over the horse, threw the biggest string vest you ever saw over it, and then towed me in her wake to the corner of the sand school where the field gate was standing open.

"We have to find Sally."

That gate, where the big hedge ended behind the byre, was on the ridge of The Brink where it ran up towards the dark flank of Foxford Wood off to the left. The roof of my cottage nestled among the hedgerows away down to the right. Ahead and below Skipley itself was not much more than a grey stain on the green patchwork that was the Warwickshire countryside. It was hard to imagine all those people working there, my husband among them. There is no rift in the world as wide as that between urban and rural living. Down there people were living on the edge of their chairs and a heart attack, and running one another down with cars and cute accounting, and up here we were searching the fields for a young woman who had fallen off a horse. At least, I presumed that was what had happened.

"Probably," agreed Karen. "Though she may have got off for some reason, and the horse pulled away and came home. In which case we'll meet her half-way up the field, and she will not be in a good temper."

I had trouble keeping up with her. She was a little taller than me, not much, and quite a lot younger, but mostly it was that half her working life was spent striding over fields in wellington boots and she knew how to do it efficiently. I alternated between clearing the tops of the grass with giant strides and stumbling over cow-pats.

The hill ran away from us like the swell of the earth's hips. Hedges interrupted it, but nothing stopped that fertile curve until it broke like a tide on the grey rocks of sterile Skipley, where the heat-haze was more than half smog. We walked across the breast of it rather than down towards the town, making for the wood.

"Would she have gone into the woods?"

Karen shook her head. "I don't think so. David never did—does . . ." Her tongue stumbled on the thing that she'd got through the last days by walking round, and it took her a moment to regain her balance. "It's not much good for riding; it's too overgrown. Besides, I don't think you can get in this way any more. There is a gate, but it's rusted up."

By now we could see most of the field, including the heavy timber obstacles, brown with creosote, clustered loosely between the hem of the wood and the bottom corner of the field. There was no sign of Sally, so she wasn't on her feet and storming after Lucy with murder in her eyes. If she was there, she was still down, behind a jump or somewhere out of sight.

"The steps," Karen said tersely, breaking into a run. I went with her.

David had used the steep slope to create a flight of giant steps, shored up with sleepers and carpeted with gravel, each of the three risers two feet high, each of the treads maybe twelve feet square. A shapeless huddle in purple and black lay at the foot of the staircase. We quickened our pace and Karen shouted her name, but there was no movement that I could see in response.

Her extra inches, her fewer years, or perhaps just her more active lifestyle brought Karen first to the foot of the steps, where she dropped on her knees beside Sally's still sprawled figure. I called sharply, "Don't move her!" and panted up in her wake, ready for broken bones at the very least.

When I touched her, she started to stir. If she'd been unconscious, she was already on her way back; perhaps she had been only stunned. Her hands made vague paddling motions towards her head. Her eyes flickered, and she looked shocked and puzzled and a little afraid. For a moment she didn't seem sure where she was or who we were.

Then slowly I saw sense creeping back into her eyes. She said, "What happened?" and her voice was reedy but with a reassuring note of irritation.

"You must have fallen off," I said. "Lie still for a moment while we see what the damage is."

"Fell off be damned," she said, quite tartly, and then, "My head hurts."

The one thing you don't do is whip off a protective helmet to see what's going on underneath. I once saw the results of some well-meaning soul doing that to a motorcyclist. He'd been conscious and talking after the accident, but when I met him, he was on a mortuary slab with his head in pieces. So I went very slowly and very cautiously, and only eased Sally's crash-hat off when I was confident that her brain wasn't going to pop out.

I put the hat, bright in its purple silk, on the grass beside us and probed gently at the tender skull under Sally's dark curly hair. I found an area of incipient swelling, but the damage was neither profound nor widespread. The hard hat had done its job of absorbing most of the force of her fall. Without it she would certainly have been a stretcher case.

"I think you'll live," I said, straightening up. Essentially unhurt, she reverted from being a patient to being a suspect again. "Can you walk, or shall I fetch a car?"

"I can walk," she said gruffly, climbing to her feet using the step behind her and a hand from Karen for support. "Where's my hat?"

Karen bent for it, and froze rigid with it in her hands, staring at it, still half-bent. She couldn't seem to speak, so I took it from her and looked for the cause of her consternation.

And found it: two holes about the size of my little finger, about four inches apart in the purple silk. They looked just like bullet holes. Under the silk the matt shell of the hat was scarred with a deep straight channel about as long. It looked just like a bullet crease.

It looked very much as if someone, having disposed of Gilgamesh's own rider, was now using similar methods to dislodged the first substitute. It looked very much as if my favourite suspect had come within an inch and a half of being the next victim.

It looked very much as if I had been wrong.

III

Harry's people combed the field with metal detectors, but they never found the bullet. They found three old horseshoes, one still with a bit of wear in it, a length of rusty chain buried in the topsoil, and a hinge.

Even with metal detectors it was always going to be a long shot —a pin in a very large haystack, there was no judging how far it had travelled or in what direction after glancing off Sally's hat— but it was a pity. Given the lump of lead, forensics could probably have confirmed that it came from the same gun which shot David. As it was, they could only look at the hat and the silk and say the damage was consistent with a .240 rifle bullet.

As the trauma of the blow and the fall began to fade, so the shock of being shot at surged towards a peak. Sally was talking to Harry about what had happened when, half-way through a sentence, suddenly she began to tremble. I made them stop for a minute, sent Karen for a mug of tea and Ellen for a warm cardigan, and only when Sally was wrapped in one and round the other and her voice was back under control did I let them continue.

Harry said, "Did you hear the shot?"

Rather carefully, Sally shook her head. "I don't remember doing. But you're surrounded by sound on top of a galloping horse, unless it was pretty close I wouldn't expect to hear it."

"You were moving at some speed, then."

She thought. "Not cross-country pace, but more than a canter. Maybe about five hundred metres a minute."

Harry, like me, grew up on the wrong side of metrification for this make any sense to him. His face went still in the middle and fell round the edges. His eyes looked put-upon. "What's that in real money?"

As we were too old to be genuinely bilingual, so Sally was too young. She wrestled with the mathematics for a moment, then made an educated guess. "About twenty miles an hour?"

Harry nodded slowly. "That's marksman standard. Unless he was lucky." I noted that the feminine pronoun had dropped out of fashion, but in all the circumstances did not feel inclined to complain. "What sort of line were you riding—what angle and which direction?"

He had brought one of the big maps up from the police station, the scale large enough to show the boundaries of individual fields. It was spread out on the coffee-table: we were gathered again in the drawing-room.

Sally leaned over it and sketched a line with a fingertip. "I was heading for the steps, going up. I'd just made the turn. As near as damn it I was heading straight for the wood."

"So he fired from either the wood in front of you or the hedge behind. The distance would be about the same; maybe the hedge is a little closer." He went to the door and spoke briskly with the constable outside. John Martin was directing the search in the field below the wood and the message was for him. Harry came back and sat down. "Did you see or hear anything while you were down the field—someone walking, perhaps, or the sound of a car—even well before the shot?"

"I really don't think so." She was trying to remember, but there didn't seem to be anything there to recall. "I don't know if it's significant, but I remember that I fell forward. Does that mean I was hit from behind?"

"Probably, though it's hard to be sure, particularly with a moving target. If your head was turned through just a few degrees at the critical moment, the shot could have been fired from a hundred yards either side of the obvious. If it's the .240 again, you're not going to be talking of a massive accurate range; but unless he's left something behind we're going to be hard put to pinpoint the place he fired from."

"Does it matter?" I asked. "I mean, if he's left nothing, does it matter where he was standing?" Even I had abandoned the feminine pronoun now.

"Hard to say," said Harry. "It might have told us something about which way he'd come, or it might not. Not knowing whodunnit from the start means us real policemen have to clutch at straws like that." It was a gentle little jibe at me, but I declined to rise. I thought I probably deserved it.

"Miss Fane," he went on, and the sudden formality meant he was serious, "until we get this character, you're obviously in danger from him. He's already put David Aston in hospital; now he's turned his attentions on you. Assuming that it is the same man and the same motive, there's no reason to suppose he'll stop until either he stops you or we stop him.

"We'll be doing the best we can, but these things can take time. In the meantime, we can protect you, but we can't protect you from a man in a hedge while you're galloping across open country.

If you'll stay indoors, either here or at Standings, we can look after you."

"Indoors?" Her chin came up pugnaciously, and outrage flared in her eyes. "How the hell do I train an eventer indoors?"

"I don't imagine you can. That's about the size of it. The horse is going to have to wait until we have this sorted out."

"Wait?" The word exploded from her. "He's a horse, not a bicycle. You can't put him away in the potting shed until next time you want him. It takes twelve weeks to get an eventer fit, and a couple of hours' work a day to keep him that way. If he misses work now, he's not going to be at Bramham and he's not going to the World Championships."

"Is there nowhere else he could go to the trained?"

"Of course," Sally said shortly. "Any yard in the country would give its tiger-trap to get its hands on Gilgamesh. How many of them could actually cope with him is another matter. But let me get this straight. You're saying he's what this is all about—Gilgamesh? That David was shot because he was trying out for the team on him, and that I was shot at in case the selectors should give me the ride?"

Put like that, it sounded absurd. Harry nodded non-committally. "That seems to be one possibility. The horse is the only direct link between David and you."

"But it wasn't him I was riding; it was Lucy."

Harry looked at me, one eyebrow cocked. But there was an explanation. I said, "It's not the horse he wants to disable; it's the rider. He didn't want to risk Gilgamesh, so he waited till you were riding something else."

Sally's eyebrows knit, trying to follow my reasoning. "Supposing we accept that. If the horse goes somewhere else to be trained; what's to stop this lunatic from following and shooting another rider off his back?"

To that question there was no answer. Harry nodded slowly. "You're right. It's not safe for anyone to ride him."

"Then he—whoever—he's won. He shot David and tried to shoot me, and we've let him win."

"Only for now. It won't feel like winning when we put him behind bars."

"But by then, it'll be too late—for Gilgamesh and for me." Her colour was coming back; so was that light like wine or madness or religion in her eye. "Let's not beat about the bush here. What happened to David was monstrous, but it's given me a chance I would never otherwise have got. It's a pretty long chance, but even if it was a dead cert and giving it up would put David back on his feet, I'd do it, and I'd do it without a second thought. But it won't, and I'm damned it I'm giving up a chance at the World Championships for no better reason than that some bastard with a gun wants me to and I don't even know why.

"Harry, I'm sorry, I know I'm making it difficult for you; I know you can't protect someone who won't be protected. I take full responsibility. But I'm not going to be beaten, not like this. If he wants Gilgamesh's place on the team, he's going to have to find a horse that's better than him; and if he wants the ride on Gilgamesh, he's going to have to be better than me."

"Or kill you."

It was a bald statement of fact, and inarguable. For a moment it set Sally back on her heels. While her head still ached, the very real danger was too close to be rationalised away. But she rallied quickly, calling perhaps on that remarkably fluid sense of balance that keeps riders on top of horses when the two are moving in dissimilar ways in bare approximations of the same direction and everything that Newton and Einstein discovered points to an early parting.

"Yes, I dare say he will try again, unless you find him first. Now I know that, I can make it harder. Get me a flak jacket. Whatever protection you can give us, concentrate on the house and yard: I'll do all my slow work in the sand school and make my fast work in the field as fast as I safely can. If we can work it that way, I'll only ride out on Gilgamesh; if he's worried about the horse, that'll maybe clip his wings a bit. I'll make it as difficult for him as I can, Harry, but unless David actually forbids me to ride his horse, I'm not going to be scared off before he's had his chance. And I've had mine."

Ellen was standing behind the sofa, very still and quiet. Sally and all of us turned to look at her. Her face was pale, her eyes deep with the shock of the recurrent nightmare. But her voice when she spoke was quite calm and deliberate. "If I thought that riding Gilgamesh would get you hurt, I would shoot him myself today. If I'd known he would get David hurt, I'd have done it last week."

Sally knelt on the shabby velvet and caught Ellen's hands over the high balding back of the sofa. "I understand how you feel that way just now. But it isn't actually true, Ellen, and if you think about it, you'll see that. Eventing is a risk sport. We all know people who've been put in hospital by their horses, who've been put in wheelchairs, who've been put under ground. We all know what we risk every time we put a foot in the stirrup. If the results weren't worth the risk to us, we wouldn't do it.

"Well, a man with a gun is a different type of risk, but the big bay bastard may still get me before he has the chance to. I'm gambling I can outwit and outmanoeuvre both of them. I may be wrong; I may wake up tomorrow or the next day in a ward across from David's, or maybe not at all. But that's a prospect I've faced daily since I first started racing crazy horses across fixed timber. The odds may be shortening, but the gamble is still the same. I want to ride him, Ellen. And if David was in the same position, he'd be set on riding him too."

After Harry had gone, Ellen called a council of war in the drawing-room. I thought perhaps she'd been waiting for him to go, in which case I should go too, and I started to make my excuses. But she called me back.

"If you're going to be here helping us, you're as involved as anyone. And for the record, I've nothing to say that I want kept from Harry. But we should work out what we're going to do, and the best and safest ways of doing it. We know how Sally feels about this. I'd like to know what Karen thinks: anything we do is likely to affect her more than anyone. I'd like to know what you think, Clio. There are different ways we can go here, but I'm not making any plans that involve anyone more than she wants to be involved. If we go on with this, there are going to be risks—for everyone, not just Sally."

As she was saying this, she was drawing the curtains. It was just after two in the afternoon. I thought it a rather dramatic gesture, but actually she was right. Someone who could shoot a girl off a galloping horse with a .240 deer rifle would have no difficulty shooting the same girl in an armchair behind an uncurtained window and from further away.

Actually, he was probably miles away right now, aware that the police would be combing the fields and woods around Foxford and content to wait, knowing that in time they must finish and go, leaving behind perhaps a sentinel or two but inevitably nothing like the ring of steel needed to keep out a skilful and determined assassin. You can protect people pretty effectively, but only by putting them in defensible places.

Just a few men can guard a high-rise hotel room round the clock. The same accommodation in a detached bungalow would need five times the cover and still be more vulnerable to a surprise attack. To defend a house like Foxford, even without extending the dragnet to the estate, would take a small army. Harry hadn't got an army. Jack Kennedy had an army, but they couldn't keep a processional route through Dallas safe for him. If he'd been content to run his presidency from a high-rise hotel room, he'd probably be alive today.

As long as his owner and his rider kept alive Gilgamesh's challenge for the World Championships, we were all in danger. Foxford was under siege, surrounded by the infinite moments of threat that one man can present when you don't know who he is.

When she had straightened the drape of the curtains, the afternoon sunshine filtered, rather than excluded, by the worn fabric,

Ellen came and sat down, the four of us forming a small conspiratorial knot round the coffee-table in the middle of the big room. Then she began speaking again, her voice quiet and serious and braced by the authority I had seen growing in her in the days since David was shot.

"It seems to me that we have three options. We can accept defeat gracefully, rough Gilgamesh off, and turn him out in a field to let this madman know he's no longer a contender, as David's ride or anyone else's. If we do that, and assuming that the horse is indeed the reason for all this, I don't expect we'll be troubled any more. We can get on with our lives and our work, and at least there'll be one less horse in the stables.

"Or we can find a yard that'll take him and train him, and put their own rider on him, and hopefully take him to the Championships. Again, if we do that, we'll probably avoid any more trouble —except for the sleepless nights we'll have worrying that we've wished our problem onto somebody else and whether Gilgamesh will get them before the gunman can." It could have been a little joke to lighten the atmosphere, but it wasn't. She was absolutely serious. She was afraid that the horse could kill someone.

"Or we can keep him in training here. The advantages are that we know we can cope with the horse: Karen can do him and Sally can ride him without any particular likelihood that he'll put them in the hospital. Also, we know what we're up against as far as this other thing goes. We've seen enough to take it seriously; no one else has to get shot before we start watching our own and each other's backs. And we already have the co-operation of our local police. Someone coming fresh to the problem in another part of the country might not get the same help, at least until someone else got hurt. You can't expect them to surround a horse with the same sort of security they provide for visiting heads of state."

We smiled and waited for her to go on. When she didn't, after a minute Sally said, "It sounds like you've already decided."

Ellen sighed. "Decided one thing anyway. I'm not going to send him away."

No one raised an argument. Clearly she was right.

When no one else spoke, Karen said, "If he's staying here and if Sally's going to ride him, I want to groom for her. I don't expect that makes me a target, but anyway I'll risk it. But the big problem isn't going to be Gilgamesh: it's the other seven horses. It's crazy for Sally to risk being shot at seven times a day riding out on horses that someone else could do quite safely. I could exercise them, enough to keep them fit anyway, but I can't ride them round the likes of Bramham, and their owners wouldn't thank me for trying.

"Unless we can get another rider in, I think we have to ask their owners to send the four that aren't ours to another yard where they can be done properly and ridden out by whoever's going to compete with them. And where they won't get caught in any cross-fire. I'm sorry, Ellen; I wanted to keep them together for David too. But I don't think we've any right to. Not if we're keeping Gilgamesh."

Ellen leaned forward and touched her hand. "You're right. I'm glad you thought of it. I'll call the four of them today, see if they can move their horses out tomorrow. They'll understand. Maybe they'll come back another season." She straightened up and smiled, not like a woman who'd just lost most of her income. "Never mind, we still have our own four. And it does solve one problem: how to manage without David and Jane."

"All right," said Sally slowly. "So I ride Gilgamesh—and Pasha, I can't leave him just standing there, but he won't need as much as the younger horses; I can do most of his work in the school—and Karen rides the other three. We can split the stable-work between us. We can do the five between two of us for as long as it takes."

My heart lifted. What, no more call for a supernumerary shit-shoveller?

Someone said, "You're not getting rid of me as easily as that," and I was amazed to find it was me. "Maybe you can manage without me now, but I want to help. There must be something I can usefully do. Hell, I can sit on the roof with a pair of binoculars and a whistle if there's nothing else going."

Ellen sat back and smiled, and there was something like pride in her face. "We're going to beat this. We're going to beat it and come through it, and I don't give a tinker's damn whether the horse gets to the World Championships, but he's damn well going to have his crack at the trials."

IV

For a week we were amazingly careful, peeping round corners before turning them and opening feed-bins as if they might be booby-trapped, and absolutely nothing happened. For the first three days, we had a police minder. Then we had a part-time minder, and a little after that we had a crunch on the gravel every few hours as a cruising squad car included us on its itinerary, between the glue-sniffers of the Chamberlain Estate and kids stoning cars off the motorway flyover. Then it was Bramham.

They travelled up to Yorkshire on the Wednesday. With half the horses away home, the only occupant of the big van was Gilgamesh. Since the other three were staying behind, Karen had to stay with them, so Ellen was both driver and groom. She invited me along for the trip, but I wanted to stay and give Karen what help and moral support I could. She was obviously disappointed to miss the big event but accepted it as unavoidable. She cheered up when she found that at least she wouldn't be entirely on her own.

Ellen phoned me on the Friday, after the dressage phase (largely satisfactory, occasionally impressive, but with momentary lapses of temper, and the horse wasn't bad either), and on the Saturday, Karen and I made an absurdly early start, raced through our chores, then piled into Harry's car to race up the M1 and beyond, in order to reach Bramham in time for Sally's cross-country. Rather to my surprise, Harry announced he was coming too. It may have been me he wanted to keep an eye on, but I think it was the car.

To my joy and surprise, there was practically no mud. There was no problem driving into the car-park and no prospect of difficulty getting out. The turf was green, not brown. The gypsy encampment of caravans no longer resembled a cluster of mosques with ranks of shoes waiting patiently around the doors. Both my yellow wellies and Harry's finding-things-in-sewers boots were redundant. Clumping round all afternoon behind me, Harry managed somehow to give the impression that this was my fault.

Before the car was stopped, Karen was out and trotting through the ranks of vehicles, pointing rather vaguely ahead of her. "I'll go and help out at the vet box." She turned round, running backwards for a pace or two, pointing another way. "If you want to watch some of the fences, your best bet's over thataway. Never mind the big personality fences with the crowds round them: find somewhere you can see three or four fences at once, then you can see how the course is riding."

That was the last we saw of her until tea-time.

We studied the programme, found Sally's number, and peered after a few galloping backs to see how long it was to her turn. Then we followed Karen's advice and traced the line of the course round until we found ourselves on the inside of a curve with a small eminence from which we could watch the horses through a wide arc and over four different obstacle. We sat down on Harry's raincoat and passed his binoculars between us.

Even those of us who love my husband dearly—three at the last count: me, his mum, and his brother, Charlie—would not pretend that he's easy to entertain. It's not that he has no capacity for enjoyment—I don't know about the other two, but I can testify unreservedly that he has—more that he has a built-in resistance to anything that comes designed and packaged for his amusement. He is either the crowning triumph of the work ethic or one of its casualties, depending on how you look at it.

His idea of relaxation is creosoting the fence. His idea of good television is watching workers blast a highway through the Amazonian rain forest. His idea of a real treat is crawling round our garage floor under his first love, the Riley—he only stopped driving it to work when an independent road test established that he'd have to give best to a bank robber making his getaway in a Reliant Robin—getting oily and smelly and occasionally crushing his thumb. But will he take it to rallies and enjoy showing it off and looking at other people's? He will not. "It's a car, not a poodle," he grunts, and disappears back under the sump.

So it was with considerable surprise, even some suspicion, that I realised he had stopped complaining about the crowds, and the walk from the car-park, and his boots, and the fact that horses kept galloping past and spoiling his view of the park, and actually seemed to be taking some interest in the competition and the competitors. He kept referring to the programme. A couple of times he clumped down the hill to stand beside particular fences and watch how different riders tackled them. I even caught him making notes in the margin, but I couldn't read them.

He said, "I'd no idea how substantial these things are."

We were looking at a pile of timber, not so much logs as tree-trunks, like giant spillikins tipped across the track. They could have been left as they had fallen off the dumper-truck, with just a little red flag added at one end and a white one at the other. There was no obvious route through. Some horses did it in two jumps at one side, others in three down the middle. One jumped into the middle and wouldn't jump out again. One, jumping the corner, misjudged the take-off and ended up spread-eagled across it with its front feet on the ground and its back ones hung up briefly on the fence. The rider, who had made a close inspection of his horse's ears while this was happening, was now upright again, looking round in some embarrassment at the interested crowd gathering. After a moment, with a wriggle and a heave, the horse sorted itself out and the combination continued, apparently none the worse for wear.

Harry said thoughtfully, "You don't realise just how powerful the horses are. Or how fast they can travel, or how few things stop them." Deep in his policeman's brain the mills were turning again, but I didn't know what they were grinding or to what end.

But they didn't grind uninterrupted for too long, because while we were standing beside the fence we found ourselves caught up in a small drama. A little black horse came sprinting down the track, turned into the fence, and got it wrong. After seeing a number of people jump it, some of them better than others but all of them managing, it was quite a shock to see somebody come a real purler.

It all happened so quickly it was hard to see exactly what had gone wrong. I think they jumped too soon, so that the horse was already coming down when it should still have been going up. Its front feet came down inside the back rail, and the impetus of its motion turned it over, literally somersaulting over the rail, its back legs stretched out and raking the sky like a child turning cartwheels. It landed on its back with a terrible crump that I could feel through the ground as well as hear and see, and the crowd round the fence sucked in a sharp breath and fell silent. I didn't know quite where the rider was at this point, but there seemed no great likelihood of either rising again.

Then with a heave and a rueful expression, the black horse got its legs under it and staggered to its feet, and a bundle of coloured silks slowly unfolded on the ground where the animal had lain. The crowd breathed again.

Someone laid a hand to the horse. It moved awkwardly for a moment, bruised by the fall, but recovered quickly, shaking off the shock and stiffness. I pushed a way through the watching cluster to where the rider was still sitting on the turf with the fence judge squatting beside her. "Can I help? I'm a doctor."

She didn't look up. "I'm all right," she said in a small voice. She was about Karen's age, frail in variegated silk. "Claire—is Claire all right?" She raised her head then and turned this way and that, looking about her with the slightly distracted air of someone who's forgotten what she's looking for and hopes she'll remember before she finds it.

"Claire?"

The fence judge smile. "The horse. It's always the horse. Claire's fine. Now what about you? Is it safe enough to move her, doctor?"

Nothing was bending the wrong way or giving her particular pain. "Oh, I think so. But have her checked out at the medical tent; she's a bit concussed."

That focused her attention faster than anything else I could have done. Her head jerked round at me, her eyes flaring. "Medical tent be damned! I'm all right. If Claire is too, we're going on."

She wasn't fit to. I touched her cheek, and the skin was cool as well as pale. There was dizziness in her eyes. It was a classic conscious concussion. "I can't advise it. You are concussed, and that means you're operating below par. If you go on, there's a strong possibility that you'll make a bad mistake before you finish, and then you or Claire might not be so lucky. Call it a day while you're both OK."

She looked at me with desperation and something akin to hatred. "Who the hell are you?"

I spread my hands defensively. "Nobody. A spectator. But I am a doctor, and I know concussion when I see it. You've had my advice; whether you take it is up to you."

"No," said the fence judge, straightening up into a young man about six feet tall, "actually it's up to me. I'm sorry, but I've no doubt the doctor is right and that leaves me with no alternative. I'm pulling you up."

"You can't!" She stumbled to her feet and stood swaying, devastation etched on her face. "You have no right!"

"As you very well know," he said calmly, "I have not only the right but the duty. If you continue with sixpence short on a shilling, you could kill yourself, your horse, a spectator—even a fence judge. I'm sorry."

"Damn you," she cried. "Have you any idea what it takes to get here—in money, time, effort, and blood? I may never make it again. What's a bit of concussion—to me, to any of us? I'm all right; I can ride on. You owe me that much."

"What I owe you," said the young man, firmly but not without sympathy, "is my job done to the best of my judgement, in your interests and everyone else's. Shouting at me isn't going to change my view that you're not fit to continue. Please pull off course and make your way back. I'll arrange a lift for you and someone to take your horse if you'd prefer."

"Leave my effing horse alone," she spat with real venom, snatching the reins from the man who held them. "I hope this happens to you one day. No, damn it, I hope you really are hurt. I hope your effing head falls off!" And with that she stumped away, trailing the horse through the interested crowd.

"Good heavens above," I said to the judge, "do they all take setbacks with such dignity?"

He grinned. "More or less. Your blood's up, you see, you couldn't do it if it wasn't. Shall I tell you something? If it does happen to me, next month at Wellesbourne say, I shall be twice as difficult and three times as rude, and every bit as ashamed of myself when I get home as she's going to be."

Harry and I walked slowly back up the hill to our vantage. "And another thing you don't realise," he said, continuing the same sentence, "is that the riders are all quite, certifiably mad."

Then it was Sally's turn. The horse before her had already been eliminated and turned for home, so we had a little wait before she appeared. But not as long as it might have been; the big horse was eating the course with great, raking strides and huge, disdainful leaps. They were all travelling fast; it was an important event and everyone entered wanted a crack at it, but the differences between the horses we had already seen and this Gilgamesh of David's were unmistakable, even to our ignorant eyes.

He couldn't have been travelling half as fast again, but he looked to be. It was as well the horse in front had pulled out, it would have been run down before the end of the course. Great muscles surging visibly under the dark shining of his coat thrust out his limbs like pistons, mechanical in their precision and tire-lessness. The sheer length of his stride devoured the ground.

It's absurd to claim I could read his expression watching from our hill—particularly as horses have bony, rather fixed faces, with only their eyes, lips, and nostrils capable of mobility. But if it wasn't an expression, it was something—in his carriage, his de-portment, his massive and overbearing presence—which told me and everyone else who saw him that day what he was feeling as he bore down on the great log-jam in his path.

It was contempt. Contempt for the fiddling little obstacles in his way. Contempt for the few scant miles he had to gallop. Contempt for the opposition, horses without his speed or strength or stamina or courage, which found themselves tested to their limits by this afternoon stroll of an event. And contempt for his rider, a blur of coloured silks perched over his shoulder, a thing of no strength without his strength, a mere passenger presuming to tell him how to gallop and how to jump—but not too often, since the price for such impertinence was to have the reins ripped out of her hands.

I had thought when they first came into view that Sally must be beating a tattoo on his ribs to make such speed. Nothing could have been further from the truth. She was sitting there—or rather crouched in her stirrups—as still as she could manage, interfering as little as she could and still keeping the horse on the track. She tried to steady fractionally for the logs, but rage glinted in the horse's eye and he snatched the rein he wanted from her and hurdled the two corners as if they'd been a couple of gorse bushes included for fun.

He treated the other fences we could see with equal disdain, and vanished from sight behind us as quickly as he had appeared. I don't think it was just us: I think the whole of the crowd gathered in that corner of the course breathed out as one and went on standing for a moment after he had passed as if aware that they had just seen something special.

"Well," said Harry after a moment, and we picked up his coat and dusted ourselves down, and clumped our way back towards the finish.

We found Ellen standing alone by the weigh-in tent, looking dazed. She brightened visibly when I hailed her, and looked up and saw us coming. "You made it, then. Harry—you too? What, are Skipley criminals taking Saturdays off now?"

"Time off for bad behaviour," murmured Harry.

Ellen grinned. "Thanks for bringing Karen. She really appreciated it; so do I."

I looked round. "She found you, then. Where is she?"

"Taking Gilgamesh back to his stall. I was happy to let her. I can't even lead that big bastard with any confidence."

"And Sally?"

"Around." She gestured vaguely. "Every time I see her she's talking to someone else. Last time it was the British *chef d'équipe*. Did you see her ride?"

"It looked a bit hairy."

"Hairy?" She shuddered. "She frightened the life out of me. To be fair though, she did a good job. I didn't think she'd be able to stay off his mouth that much, leave that much to him. It takes some nerve to sit on top of some lunatic horse galloping into a fixed fence and not try to pull him back."

"I wouldn't have thought nerve was one of Sally's problems," said Harry, and Ellen shook her head in awe and admiration.

"You can say that again."

I said, "How are they placed, then? They'll not be beaten on speed, surely."

"Not unless someone's found a way of fitting a turbo-charger. Theirs is the fastest time of the day so far—by twenty-four seconds! And that in spite of a run-out three from home. It wasn't Sally's fault; he was still travelling so fast she couldn't turn him into the last element and he just skimmed past it. That was their only mistake on the course. She retook it and was still way inside the time, but the twenty penalties will keep her out of the ribbons."

She looked at me quite sharply then, as if she'd read my thoughts. "But no, not off the team, if anybody has a notion to put her there. It was an excellent performance for a combination that's only been together a fortnight. It must have sharpened the selectors' interest in her. Nobody's seen her ride a top-class horse before; Pasha in his day was good, but he wasn't in the same league. If she can do this with Gilgamesh after a fortnight, they'll want to know what she can do with him in two or three months."

There was a kind of edge on her voice that I don't think she was aware of, that she would have blunted if she had been. It was quite a day for Foxford, for Gilgamesh and the team producing him. Even I felt some of the glow entering my soul. But it was impossible for Ellen to divorce her pleasure at the way the horse had run from the awareness that it should have been David on him, not a girl who'd had the chance of him and had to give him up because she wasn't good enough and who could never have got him here but for David's hard work and now David's tragedy. It was hard for her, in the circumstances, not to resent Sally's success.

I saw her shake herself almost physically. "I'm going to go and find a phone, and call the hospital. David will want to know how they got on."

"Give him our love," I said.

Soon after that we had to leave. It was a long way back to the Midlands, and even though Colonel Fane's lad had seen to their lunch, the remaining inmates of the stables—David's three and Pasha—were complaining of starvation and neglect by the time we returned to Foxford. I was going to stay and help, but Karen insisted she could whip through four meals and four beds in the time it would take us to drive the last half-mile home.

Until Ellen and Sally returned after the final show-jumping phase the next day, Karen would be sleeping in the house alone. Before we said good night, Harry scribbled our home phone number on the back of a card and gave it to her.

"With both Sally and Gilgamesh away, I can't see much prospect of you being bothered," he said. "But be careful, lock up properly, and if you're anxious for any reason, however silly, call us and we'll be up the hill before you've put the phone down."

"I'll be fine," she promised. She was about twenty years old and she was humouring the wrinklies. Then she grinned. "And if I'm not, I'll be down that field and hurdling the hedge into your back garden before you've time to pick the phone up!"

So we left her to her feed scoop and her shavings fork and went home. I was pleased to find that I remembered it quite clearly. There was a dodgy moment as we went past Miss Withinshaw's just as she was taking Podgy for his constitutional, but after that I had no doubt which was our gate and remembered our front door quite distinctly.

We had cocoa, a wrinkly drink if ever there was one, and then I went to bed, leaving Harry poring over his large-scale map of Skipley and environs. When I asked what he was doing, he grunted.

"And a good night to you too, dear," I said, and went up.

v

The next day was Sunday, and we went for a walk. It was Harry's idea. He said he'd walk up to Foxford with me, and when I'd finished helping Karen, we'd go for a walk in Foxford Wood. We had lived within sound of its rooks for over a year and never yet taken the trouble to walk there, but it was a nice idea and a nice day and I agreed readily enough. Besides, it was about as romantic as Harry ever gets and I didn't want to discourage him.

Listening to the gossip in the coffee shops—well, all right, transport cafes—of Skipley, you'd think you couldn't venture into Foxford Wood without tripping over writhing bodies pale in the dappled light. You'd think that parking would be such a problem in the narrow track leading there that a small multi-storey car-park would be the only solution. You'd think half the population of the West Midlands had been conceived there.

So it was something of a disappointment to find Harry and I had the place to ourselves that sunny Sunday morning. Another couple might have taken advantage of such an opportunity; but Harry's a policeman.

The wood was a lot bigger than I'd thought. We saw the face of it, where it frowned down on grey Skipley, and it ran along the northern edge of The Brink and up to the ridge that was the crown of that geological feature. What we couldn't see from our cottage, from Foxford, or from down in the valley was how it flowed smoothly over the top of The Brink and for some considerable distance down the gentler slope on the southern side. I wouldn't know an acre from a hole in the wall, let alone these newfangled hectares, but I doubt there was much change from a mile in either direction. It was a big wood, and under its canopy it was a pretty dark wood too. Any number of babes could have been lost there, any number of sharp-eyed, patter-footed, whistling Wild Wooders could have lurked among the boles and thick roots.

In a timid, Moly sort of voice I said, "Oh Ratty, I'm so glad you're here." But, of course, Harry had been boning up on the Police Manual while the rest of us were reading *The Wind in the Willows* and thought I was being silly and really rather offensive.

Tracks and paths of all proportions, from one-way hedgehog runs to rides that would have taken a robust small car, crossed and recrossed the wood. The trees themselves were spaced somewhat randomly, but at natural rather than monoculture-forestry intervals. Trees that had been allowed to grow old gracefully and die on their feet now lay rotting gently across the paths, and new paths had been worn round them. Clearly they would remain there until there was nothing more than enriched humus to feed the new generations of oak, ash, and beech. They were in no one's way, unless maybe the owner of the small car with the remarkable springs. Certainly they had not impeded the motor-cyclists who had left their tyre tracks here, baked into the dried earth round the fallen trunks and right over the top of one.

Harry studied that particular spoor, the tread deep and clearly etched in the mud either side of the tree and just a narrow track skinned of moss and crumbling bark over the top, for some time without speaking.

There were other tracks too, similarly preserved by the winter's mud drying into the long spring: a horse, a small pony, several different boots and shoes, several different dogs, a probable fox, and something heavy and clawed that I decided on no evidence at all was a badger. None of them appeared to be recent. We weren't leaving any trail that we could see, and it was unlikely that anything else in this wood in the last few weeks had either.

Harry nodded at the hoofprints. "David?"

"I doubt it. Karen says he never rides here. If he does anything like Sally's speed, I'm not surprised. You could run into a tree very handily."

"Well, someone's had a horse in here."

"Maybe someone who rides slower than your average eventer."

"Like Dick Turpin, you mean?"

"Or Paul Revere."

Harry's brow creased thoughtfully. "Was that him in the Derby?" I told you, a sense of humour. A strange sense of humour, but a sense of humour just the same.

We walked on, bearing approximately north. Harry chose the route, walking two paces ahead of me like the Queen and making increasingly rare essays at conversation. I couldn't see what was guiding him, what dictated one path rather than another as pretty and clearer. But plainly he had something in mind, so I tagged along, largely uncomplaining, although I made an exception when I found myself trailing two steps behind him through a bramble bush.

But then the dappled shade under the trees began to brighten, and we saw daylight ahead where the wood gave way at last to open fields. We walked towards the light until barbed wire stopped us, some three generations of it tangling rustily along the edge of the wood to waist height. Brambles had grown up through it; stakes supported it at irregular intervals and angles. It was more than unpassable; it was unapproachable.

We tracked left and walked until we came to a gate, but it wasn't much better: angle-iron rusted along the top to lethal points and projections, secured by a chain whose padlock might have opened once but hardly within living memory.

We stood at the impassable gate, looking down the green hill onto Skipley. Away to the right was a thick fuchsia hedge that looked vaguely familiar and a ridge-pole and a chimney-pot.

"I can see our roof!"

"Good heavens," said Harry indulgently, "even from down there?"

I glared at him, mostly from habit. "This is the field below Foxford, where David has his cross-country jumps. Where Sally was shot at."

"Where you found Sally, yes," he agreed. "Come on, this is supposed to be a walk." He led the way back into the wood, putting the field and Skipley beyond it at our backs.

At least now he stuck pretty much to the tracks, and the better ones at that, so that although the depth of the wood from front to back was further than we had walked from the lane to the rusty gate, the going was easier and the way more pleasant. But I had long since given up on the fiction of a Sunday morning stroll. It wasn't part of Harry's style. Too much of his working life had been spent on his feet for him to consider it a recreation now. His preferred exercise for Sunday mornings involved a quite different part of his anatomy.

And if it wasn't a recreational and romantic stroll with his wife in sylvan surroundings on a sunny Sunday morning at the end of May, then he was working. I sighed resignedly and tramped on in his wake. I should have known better. Perhaps I did.

In due course the woods ahead of us lightened again, and glints of a jewel-like green startled eyes grown accustomed to the dim. As we came to the southern edge of the wood, bit by bit the Shires spread their panorama before us. The slope ran away from us in a long and gentle curve, rolling like the surface of a quiet green sea towards a horizon gone to mauve with the distance. We could see hills that must have been twenty miles away: Edge Hill, the Cotswolds, even the faint blue bulk of the Malvern Hills like a backdrop painted on the sky.

Closer than that the folds of the earth were full of secret places. Little spinneys clustered in some, old houses in others. The tithe barn at Clayton, reroofed in living memory but essentially dating back to when medieval taxes were paid in kind, was a dominant feature of the view to the west, its great size in no way diminished by the manor, farm, and trees that grew up round it later or indeed by the four miles between Clayton and Foxford Wood.

More to the south and closer was the warm brickwork of Standings, rising out of a little copse of landscape planting, its outline as militarily precise and upright as the Colonel himself, a retired brigadier of a house with pink, scrubbed cheeks, whistling "Land of Hope and Glory" with the wind through its crenellations.

A little eastward lay the mill house which Jan Parker and her brother had converted, fronted with white board of doubtful authenticity but great charm and topped with a cricketing weathervane. The Maudsleys' house was down there too, a little further east and a little further away. I couldn't see the house, but the tip of the flagpole at the end of the long lawn stood proud of the surrounding trees. I had it on good authority that Mr. Maudsley ran the Union Jack up that pole twice a year, on the Queen's Birthday and St. George's Day.

It was impossible to look out over this garden of middle England and not be amazed that the mile that would take you from this edge of the wood down past the sunny pink timelessness of Standings and on the way to Clayton's ancient barn would take you from the other edge of the wood down past the hospital, over the ring road, and into Skipley, where the rain either threatened or fell almost constantly, where the grey streets were host to nameless crimes and unmentionable vices, where the very name The Black Country seemed to have been coined.

It was a landscape of extraordinary contrasts, of great beauty and great squalor, some of England's most soul-destroying towns, set in some of its most exquisite country and surrounded by some of its most delightful villages. But who sings abroad the fame of the Slaughters, Upper and Lower, of Evesham and Bourton and Broadway and Warwick? Transplant any one of them to the south coast or the Thames valley and the tourists would cram in until the little places would start to suffocate in the crush and people queueing for the public conveniences would only live long enough to reach their goal by barbecueing a passing poodle in the car-park. But whoever takes holidays in the Black Country?

So who's complaining? If word got out about the beauty of the rolling shires behind The Brink, the first thing that would happen would be that the roads authority would straighten out all the lanes—Miss Withinshaw's Podgy becoming an early casualty of the increased traffic and speed—and then they'd carve through the farmland with a branch motorway from the sinuous slumbering giant all but hidden in the distance and its own fumes away to the east. Fame has its price, for beautiful places as well as people. I just wish that friends wouldn't pat my hand consolingly when I tell them I've moved to the Midlands.

"You're a doctor," said Harry, as if he'd heard it somewhere. "How long would it take a fit man to run from down there, up this hill, through the wood, and along to Foxford?"

I looked at him. "How long is a piece of string?"

He looked at me. "I don't find that enormously helpful."

"It depends what you mean by down there. It depends what you mean by a fit man."

Harry considered. "Well—just for the sake of the argument, you understand—take Bobby Parker. He's a professional athlete but not a runner. If he heard that, say, the MCC were offering a three-year contract to the first cricketer to reach Foxford, how long would it take him on foot?"

I let my eyes play over the distance, then back to Harry. My nose wrinkled with disfavour. "You don't think Bobby—"

"No, of course not," he said briskly. "He's got an alibi, hasn't he? But all the same—"

It was perhaps half a mile from the mill house to where we were standing, a mile or a little more through the wood and along its face to Foxford. "A top-class track athlete on level going would do a mile and a half in about seven minutes. A fell runner would cope better with the slope and the going, but he'd be slower—I don't know by how much. And he'd waste a lot of time getting into and out of the wood without shredding himself on the wire."

Harry nodded sagely. "That's a very good point." He turned his back on the superb vista, not with regret but with smugness. "Well, we'd better be getting back now."

For a long time I tramped behind him in silence, glowering at the self-satisfied look on the back of his neck. I knew he was waiting for me to ask about the relevance of his questions and forbore to give him the gratification. But in time my curiosity outweighed my reluctance and I swallowed my pride with hardly a hiccup. "You don't really think someone ran over The Brink in order to shoot David?"

He stopped and turned round, smiling happily. "No, as a matter of fact I don't. But it's an interesting comparison, isn't it? A fast runner could get from Standings to Foxford in not much longer than it takes by car."

I couldn't see what he was getting at. "It's a lot shorter as the crow flies than it is by road." The map must have told him as much. But it didn't get us anywhere. Time had stopped being a limiting factor when Sally became the gunman's second victim. And how far could he have run, carrying a heavy coat and a rifle? True, he might have run away, but probably only as far as the car waiting for him at the wood or elsewhere in the lanes.

Finally Harry condescended to share his train of thought. "If a four-minute-miler could do the distance in seven minutes and a fell runner in rather more, I bet an event horse that isn't even at full stretch at twenty miles an hour could do it in under six minutes. A four-minute-man does fifteen miles per hour. I bet those horses we were watching yesterday were doing twice that across open country. With the jumps, maybe they'd average twenty-five; that's a mile and a half in well under four minutes. Allow extra for negotiating the wood, and there's still time."

I felt myself staring at him with an intensity that should have left scorch marks. "Time for what?"

"Time for Sally to ride from Standings to Foxford, shoot David, and ride back again in time to join her guests before the end of the news."

VI

I stared and stared, and for minutes on end found nothing to say. Then I sat down heavily on a fallen log. I didn't know it was there; if it hadn't been, I think I'd have sat down heavily just the same. Harry regarded me kindly for a moment. Then he sat down beside me.

At length I said weakly, "But—Sally was shot too."

"Sally's hat was certainty shot," said Harry. "It was not necessarily on her head at the time."

What was he thinking? That she'd ridden Lucy out of the yard with a gun secreted on her person? That once down at the field she had dismounted, stuck her hat on a fence post, and shot it? Then, as the horse ran away, she had somehow disposed of the gun, crammed the hat back on her head and arranged herself artistically at the foot of the stairs, pausing only to hit herself on the head in order to produce the realistic swelling and other signs of trauma? It was incredible, literally. But I couldn't think of any more convincing scenario.

Harry could. Harry had. And he hadn't done it all in the last hour as we walked in the wood. Our Sunday stroll had not been to develop a theory but to test one.

"She could have done it the night before. Nobody heard a shot; it was just the horse coming home that alerted you. She could have shot the hat previously, taking as much time and care as she needed, and then put the gun back wherever she keeps it. All she had to do in the field was get off the horse, give herself a bang on the head—not enough to knock herself out, just enough to produce the bruise—and lie down. You and Karen did the rest."

"She wouldn't risk riding out with a hole in her hat. One of us would have noticed. At least, there was every chance that we would."

"Yes—sorry," said Harry. "She had to change the silk cover too. She had two the same colour: the perforated one was in her pocket when she rode out, and she changed them over in the field. The other one was in her pocket when you found her, but who was going to search her pockets then, and what matter if she was carrying a spare silk? She was taking it home to wash it or something."

I was thinking about it, catching up slowly with the intellectual and emotional implications of what he was saying. The mind got there first. What he was saying would work. There were no practical obstacles to belief—maybe some details to resolve, but nothing fundamental. She could have done it.

The heart took longer. Once I had been convinced of Sally's guilt. After the incident with the hat seemed to disprove it, perhaps in compensation I had found myself warming to her tough, determined, courageous manner. Of course, if there was no gunman, there was a lot less to be courageous about.

The heart was getting there. "If she did that, she shot David."

"Yes. She knew she was under suspicion, even if it was only a casual one. The best way to avoid being considered as the culprit was to become a victim. It worked on you, didn't it?"

I had to admit that it had. I had considered it conclusive, inarguable. "Not you?"

He shrugged. "You made a good case against her. You were right: too many things slotted together for it to be only coincidence. After it seemed she'd been shot at, you felt guilty about suspecting her and didn't think any more about it. I'm paid to be a nasty suspicious bastard and when I thought it through, it was still possible it was her—if she could travel quickly enough between Standings and Foxford. Well, across country on an event horse—

and if Pasha isn't among the top flight, I would guess he's still good enough—she could. It becomes possible that she shot David. If she made the holes in her own hat, it's certain."

"My God." I couldn't think of anything else to say.

"Yes," he said. "I know."

"Sally. Sally shot David?"

Harry nodded. "I think so."

"Sally Fane shot David Aston because she wanted to ride his horse? It's incredible!"

He laughed aloud at that, which was a little unkind if wholly understandable. "That's what I said. I was wrong. You were right all along."

"Sally. How could she?"

"Greed. Most crimes are committed for it. People wanting more of something than they're entitled to: more money, more miles per hour, more freedom, more love, more future. Sally wanted the chance David had worked for, and she didn't much care what she had to do to him to get it."

I took a deep breath and let it out again slowly, and the wood stopped wobbling round me. "The wood though. She had to get the horse through here to make the time, but I don't know how. That gate hasn't been opened for years."

"She jumped. Either the gate or the wire: neither of them is that high."

I shook my head. I had the sensation of something slipping out through my fingers like dry sand, and for the life of me I couldn't have said if that was frustration or relief I felt. "The height isn't the problem. Not every obstacle is jumpable. You need—" I groped round in my memory for facts. You can pick up a lot in just a few weeks, but I had no framework of basic knowledge on which to hang what I had learnt and it made recall harder. "You need an approach, and somewhere to land, and clearance over the jump for your head and the horse's. You need well-defined top and groundlines to the jump or the horse can't judge it. They can't jump wire at all because they don't see it in time to take off."

We walked back to the gate. Looked at in that light, it seemed even less passable than before. The landing into David's field was fine. The height was fine: it was higher than the cross-country fences but so much lower than the gate out of the sand school which I had seen Gilgamesh hurdle that I supposed it well within the scope of a competent eventer such as we knew Pasha to be.

There the pros ended and the cons began. The top of the gate was rusted to a series of jagged points connected only occasionally by the fragments of a top bar. The bottom was lost in undergrowth that, like the chain securing it, hadn't been disturbed for years. Because of the trees growing near it, the only possible approach was at an acute angle, and even then the horse would have to jump with no rider to help or encourage him, except vocally from the low branches where she would undoubtedly be hanging.

I looked at it and I shook my head. "Harry, I'm only a three week expert in this, but I don't think it's on. I don't see how she could jump that."

Harry didn't either. He said doubtfully, "It's that or the wire."

"No. It's that or the wire, or we're wrong."

He considered, then said pontifically, "It's that, or the wire, or we're wrong, or she found some other way of doing it."

"What about the hoofprints? Somebody rides in here; they must have got in somehow."

"Up the lane, like us. Anyone could ride in the wood, but only someone who could jump in and and then jump out again could get from Standings to Foxford in six minutes."

We were still standing at the gate, glaring at it for its unwarranted intrusion into a perfectly good theory, when the moon-white shape that was Lucy, her snake-like head and neck low as she loped over the ground with strides so long they appeared almost slow, cantered into view. It was the first time I'd seen Karen ride her outside the confines of the sand school. I doubt she'd have been doing it now, except that David was in hospital and Sally was in Yorkshire, and Lucy hadn't stretched her legs over turf for five days.

I imagine she was a good enough rider to manage at all, but she hadn't Sally's skill and she hadn't Sally's confidence, and the other thing was that she rode as if the horse was a friend, a thing of blood and bone and feelings and some intelligence. Sally rode the same horse as if it was a tool, a conveyance, a biological machine. It occurred to me that thinking of people in much the same way, as animate instruments of her own will, would have made possible what she had done. She didn't hate David when she shot him, any more than she hated Lucy when she jabbed her mouth and sides with demanding steel. She had a use for them both, and saw or chose to see no further than that. The medical profession, which is sometimes better at naming conditions than curing them, has a word for people who think like that. It calls them psychopaths.

I waited, watching, for the sweep of the horse's progress round the field to bring her up towards the wood, and then for a break in the thunder of her stride that would let my voice through. "Karen. We're over here."

I saw that she had heard me by the way her body straightened abruptly out of its jockey's crouch and her head turned all ways as she sought the source of the hail. Her face, in the moment before she saw me waving and recognised me, was afraid. Remorse stabbed at me. The last time she'd been in this field she'd found the apparent victim of a shooting.

"Karen, it's me—Clio. We're over here at the gate."

Fast on recognition came embarrassment. Between the chin-strap and peak of her hard hat her cheeks were pink. She rode over and reined in. "What are you doing in there?"

Harry was bent almost double, inspecting the foot of the gate where it was firmly embedded in years of undergrowth. He gave it a morose rattle. "Detecting."

I said, "Somebody's been riding in here. Who would that be—any idea?"

"Local kids with ponies. In the winter people use the wood for exercise sometimes rather than chew up their fields."

"How would they get in?"

She looked surprised. The answer was, after all, obvious enough. "Up the road and along the lane. The same way you did. Why?"

I took the easy way out. "We're arguing. Harry thinks an event horse ought to be able to jump in and out. I said horses can't jump wire."

"Well," she amended doubtfully, "some can. To some extent you can teach them, but it's always a big risk. They're forever making mistakes, even with jumps they can see clearly. If they misjudge a log they bump a fetlock. If they misjudge wire they can end up with cuts that literally never heal. Now many people want to risk that."

Harry straightened up. "So what about hunting? Hunts must be constantly meeting barbed wire."

"They do," said Karen. "And most of the horses standing in fields with their legs carved up are hunters. Not many are eventers."

Would she have risked it, even so? She had intended to cripple a man: would she have risked crippling her horse as well? Perhaps she might if she had wanted Gilgamesh so badly. But she needed Pasha to complete the task, and she needed to leave no clues to what she had done and how. Pasha with ripped knees in stable and chestnut hairs on the wire between Standings and Foxford, she absolutely could not risk.

"Mostly what they do," said Karen by way of an afterthought, "is make hunt fences."

"Hunt fences?"

She nodded. "If there's a lot of wire in their country, they make jumpable places in the fences round about. It doesn't take much. A couple of planks nailed across the wire between one fence post and the next makes it quite safe. The horses can see what they have to do then, and even if they make a mistake, they're not going to get cut. Planks, poles, a few branches cut from a hedge, even a sheet of plywood leaned up against the wire: they use all sorts. I've seen whole fields jumping over a bit of tarpaulin hung over a wire fence before now. Half the horses thought their last hour had come, but I don't think any of them touched it."

I looked at Harry and he was walking along the wire fence with measured tread and slowly, slowly smiling. "Well, that seems to settle the—um—argument. I'm glad we bumped into you. Good heavens," and he held up his wrist without bothering to look at it, "is that the time? Come on, Clio, we have to move. See you again, Karen."

And with that he turned and ambled purposefully back into the wood, leaving Karen and I to exchange a puzzled, slightly embarrassed smile. I said, "Stick to horses," not wholly in jest, and she grinned and I trotted off in his wake, feeling like an abbreviated Watson in pursuit of a more than usually obfuscatory Holmes.

"Now what are we looking for?" I asked when I caught up.

"Holes."

"Holes?"

"Holes."

It wasn't that he didn't want to tell me. He just wanted to be coaxed. "Any particular kind of holes, or are you not fussy?"

His smile was sunny. "Little ones, probably in pairs at the top of adjacent fence posts. There were two little holes at the top of that post you were leaning on, and funnily enough there were two more just like them at the top of the post next to it."

She had nailed a rail over the wire to make a fence she could jump. She may have done it days or weeks before she needed it— who would notice, and if anyone noticed, who would care?—and returned later to pull it down. She had probably used it for firewood. The stigmata of the nails would be the only evidence.

She had been very clever. You had to give her that. She had been very clever, very well prepared, and utterly cold-blooded in the planning of her crime.

But we could find no corresponding holes in the fence posts on the south side of the wood, though we trawled up and down, inside and out, for an hour. We narrowed the search to a stretch on a fairly direct route between the two houses which included the only approachable lengths of wire, but we couldn't find any physical sign that we were on the right track. Still, we would have gone on looking, Harry sidling in one direction and me in the other, if he hadn't found a viable alternative.

We were walking back towards one another again when I saw him break his stride and pause, and lean over the nettles to pluck something from the barbs of the wire.

I quickened my pace. "Found something?"

"Wool." He looked up, his brow wrinkled in perplexity, turning the stuff carefully in his fingers. "This . . . *means* something to me." The effort to remember added new creases to his already homely face.

"A three-day-event sheep?"

"No." He didn't even smile. "Not fleece; it's—"

By then I was beside him and could see what it was: two or three strands of grey woollen fibre, slightly felted in appearance, wool from a woven rather than a knitted fabric.

"Army blankets," I said.

Harry looked at me as if I was mad. "What?"

"Army blankets. My dad was in the Army during the war. By means I wot not of, he came home afterwards with two Army blankets. I slept under one of them for years. They felt just like that. They were even that colour."

"You think she threw an Army blanket over the wire?" He had every right to sound doubtful.

"Colonel Fane got his rank from somewhere."

Harry's left eyebrow climbed. "You want me to march down there and ask Colonel Fane if he was involved with your dad in an Army-blanket black market?"

"On the other hand, it could be the stuff they line stable rugs with."

VII

So we walked down through the fields to Standings to ask the Colonel if his daughter had a jute rug lined with grey blanket.

It was a difficult interview. I wondered if it would be easier without me there, just man to man, but decided the only one it would be easier for was me and so stayed.

Nor was it made less difficult by the fact that when he saw us coming across the lawn behind his home, the Colonel thought we had come over to congratulate him on his daughter's performance at the event.

He was in the sitting-room at the back of the house and saw us through the high casements, with their long, white glazing bars like impossibly slim fingers pointing out the finer details of the architecture. If he thought there was anything strange about rather distant neighbours approaching his house via a wood, three fields, and his back lawn, nothing in his greeting indicated as much. He raised a hand and waved us up, and met us at the conservatory door.

"Walked over from Foxford? Great heavens, that must be a couple of miles. Come in, sit down, take some refreshment. What will you have? I can recommend Mrs. Handcock's lemonade if it's a little warm for sherry."

We accepted the lemonade. It was cool and sharp, opaque with the fragments of flesh and rind spiralling in it like sea-gulls riding a thermal. The Colonel sat down with us on the cast-iron chairs in the conservatory, his long, scrubbed, perfectly shaved cheeks pink with pleasure.

"That was a splendid idea of yours, going up to Bramham yesterday. Did you see anything of Sally's ride?" We nodded. "Excellent! How was she going?"

Harry said, "Like a bat out of hell." I noticed how low his voice was. I don't think the Colonel did.

"Splendid. Of course, they put up the fastest time of the day, even with the run-out. Without that they'd have been the combination to beat. After less than three weeks together again it was a damn good showing." He chuckled then, his sharp blue eyes twinkling. "Forgive me. I'm not only a proud father in this; I'm a proud breeder. It doubles the likelihood of becoming a bore on the subject."

Harry said, "How long is it since you sold David the horse?"

The Colonel looked at him a little oddly but answered amiably enough. "It must be nearly four years now. We had him till he was five. Sally broke him, of course, so it was easier for her to get on terms with him again than for somebody starting afresh. At least, that's what we hope the selectors will think."

"You must wish now that you'd kept him."

The sharp gaze wasn't softening at all. Colonel Fane knew that, however politely, however tactfully, he was being questioned. He was helping police with their enquiries. The flush of pleasure died from his cheeks. But he answered Harry's questions adequately and accurately, partly because he saw no reason not to, partly because he respected the tradition of law even when its practice was personally inconvenient, but mostly I think because our visit had made him our host and he accepted that certain obligations came with that. One was that he shouldn't tell us to go boil our heads. He might have thought it; he might even have conveyed something of the thought in the precise angle of an eyebrow, the exact note of a word; but we'd have to be a lot more personal and offensive yet before he'd tell us to mind our own damn business.

I sighed inwardly. Where we were going was about as personal and offensive as you could get, but by the time we got there the Colonel would have no illusions left about our respective roles. However testy the host became, the guests wouldn't leave in a huff until the purpose of the visit had been achieved.

"You can't keep them all," he said. "Besides which, as a breeder, your aim is to put horses where they will do the best they're capable of. You're judged on the competition results of your progeny. That horse has gone further with David Aston than he would have done if he'd stayed with us."

"Does Sally share your view?"

The eyes were like steel-blue needles now, the voice honed to a perfect silky edge. "I would have thought my daughter's views would be something you would discuss with her."

"I'm sorry, Colonel. I'd like to have your opinion." Harry's voice was quiet, firm, both respectful and sympathetic. I knew he was a cleverer man than most people realised, and a kinder one. I tended to lose track of his enormous professionalism. Even through the strain of the situation I got a little lift from being reminded.

Colonel Fane regarded him levelly, containing his anger but not so completely that we were unaware of it. "Very well. Yes, I imagine"—the word was selected, not arbitrary—"that she has mixed feelings on the subject. She's proud of the horse and fond of David, but if we could turn the clock back, I imagine she'd choose to keep the animal. Even so, she might not have succeeded with him. With some horses, and Gilgamesh is that sort, there's only one possible combination for success. At the time, we thought his temperament would always be too much of an albatross round the neck of his talent. She was getting better results with Pasha, so when I got David's offer for the bay, I took it. Sally was sorry to see him go, but the economics of the business depend on selling horses, and you don't get far only selling the bad ones. And then—" He stopped.

"And then?" prompted Harry.

The Colonel's quiet anger was growing to real resentment, but still he answered. "This was nearly four years ago—before David was married, before his father died. David and Sally knocked around together a lot when they were teenagers. They shared the same interests, went the same places. There weren't many other youngsters living on The Brink at that time—I'm not sure there were any—so naturally they enjoyed each other's company. I used to think David spent more time here than he did at home, but

Reggie Aston assured me he was always tripping over the pair of them at Foxford.

"Both of us rather assumed that when they were old enough, they'd—well, do something about it. But time went on and nothing much happened. They remained friends, but as they got about more, they saw less of one another. Then David met Ellen at a shooting party and three months later they were married."

Harry said slowly, "So when you sold him the horse, you were thinking of David as almost part of the family."

"Yes, that's true."

"And aware in your own mind of the possibility that he might actually be part of your family at some point in the future?"

"As I said," the Colonel said stiffly, "both David's father and I half-expected and were perfectly happy with the idea of them marrying."

"Was Sally half-expecting it too?"

At that the Colonel's head came up like that of a rearing horse, and his cold eyes flashed a warning. "That really is something you'll have to take up with my daughter!"

"Fair enough," Harry said reasonably. "OK, three more questions. You said Ellen Aston can shoot. Can Sally?"

"Of course. I taught her myself. She's very good."

"Have you ever known anyone—particularly David or Sally when they were kids—ride across Foxford Wood, between your fields and that big field of David's?"

Fane's eyes widened, but he thought about it and then he remembered. "Yes, David did it once. On a good hunting pony he had. The wood wasn't just as overgrown then; Reggie took timber out regularly for firewood and for sale. David would have been about thirteen. He piled branches up against the wire on both sides and timed himself between his house and ours. If I think for a minute I'll even remember how long it took him."

"Think for a minute," said Harry.

"Five minutes and forty-two seconds," said the Colonel. "Sally wanted to try it too, but I wouldn't let her. She hadn't David's pony, she hadn't David's skill, and even in those days she had more guts than was good for her."

So it was possible. Not only that, it had been done before. I breathed softly, letting it sink in.

Harry moved on briskly. "Finally, what colour is the wool lining your stable rugs?"

The utter absurdity of the question took some of the tension out of the air. Fane barked a sudden laugh, and if it was inappropriate, it was at least something of a relief. "What kind of a damn fool question is that? What colour is the gear-stick in your car? What colour are the linings of your pockets? Why would anyone even notice the colour of the inside of a jute rug?"

So, of course, we had to go and look.

With most of Colonel Fane's stock now out on the spring grazing, the rugs were piled in a neat stack in a corner of the tackroom. We carefully rifled through them, lifting successive corners. They weren't all lined with blanketing: some of the nylon ones had a fleecy lining. But there were several jute rugs and a couple of green tarpaulin jobs which were lined with thick, slightly felted wool indistinguishable from the Army blanket I slept under as a child.

Except that they weren't grey. They were fawn. They were brown. One was a tartan in near fluorescent blues and greens clearly designed for the Queen's Very Own Highlanders. None of them was lined in grey, or a grey mixture, or a mixture with just a bit of grey in it.

"Damn," said Harry.

The Colonel viewed him with entirely natural satisfaction. "Found what you're looking for?"

Harry managed an amiable smile and shook his head. "No."

Perhaps disarmed by such frankness, Fane softened his guard a little. "For heaven's sake, Marsh, tell me what you're looking for and then I can help you find it."

Harry sighed. "I'm still doing what I've been doing for the last three weeks, Colonel: looking for some explanation of what happened to David Aston. And I still haven't found it."

"You seriously think Sally could have had something to do with it?" His tone was incredulous. Almost he thought it was too silly to worry about.

"What I think doesn't matter," said Harry. "It's what I can prove that counts, and to date I have no proof against anyone."

"And in the search for proof," asked the Colonel, sharp eyes shrewd, "have you visited anyone else's tack-room?" Harry didn't answer, which I suppose was answer enough. "I don't understand you, man. You *know* she was here the night David was shot. Even if my testimony is suspect, you have four unbiased witnesses to confirm it. How could she have been at Foxford shooting David, even if she'd wanted to?"

I could see Harry debating with himself whether he should say any more. Whether it would do more harm or good depended more on the character of the Colonel than the nature of the information.

He decided. "For about ten minutes either side of the shooting Sally was not with you or within sight or earshot of you. It makes it feasible, just."

Whatever Sally Fane had or had not done, her father was neither party to it nor aware of it. He still didn't look shocked, or horrified, or grief-stricken or guilty. He looked amazed. "She was upstairs changing her dress! She spilt coffee on it."

"Whose idea was the dinner party?"

"I don't know. We'd both of us talked about having some friends round."

"Who talked about it first?"

Fane shook his head. "I really don't remember."

"All right. Were any of your staff still on the yard by ten o'clock?"

"I don't think so. We didn't have a foaling that night. I can't swear to it, but I'd expect the last of them to be away home about eight. That would be the normal thing."

"Do either you or Sally have, or have access to, a .240 deer rifle?"

"Not now. At least, we don't have one and I don't have access to one. You'd better ask Sally if she can borrow one." His moustache bristled as his lip curled. "I wouldn't necessarily know, and I'd hate to mislead you."

"Good enough. If she had the use of such a gun, would she be reasonably accurate with it?"

The moustache stood to attention. "Of course. I'll tell you something more. If she'd shot David Aston, with a deer rifle or an air pistol or a popgun, he'd be dead."

We left then, by the main gate. As we walked up the drive, followed by an almost tangible aura of resentment, Harry said quietly, "By the same token, if she intended only to disable him, she was good enough to do it."

But the interview wasn't quite over after all. As we neared the high wrought-iron gates, framing another superb view of Warwickshire in their open arch, Colonel Fane called after us, and we stopped and turned back.

He didn't give us time to reach him. It wasn't more conversation he wanted. He called testily to us, "Pasha's rug, of course, is on Pasha's back over at Foxford. I've no idea what colour it is inside, but I'd rather you look than think we have something to hide."

After the morning's exertions I couldn't face the long walk back to Foxford. We borrowed a phone and Harry called his office, and a few minutes later the squad car which was still making occasional fly-bys picked us up in the lane and drove us round to Foxford.

Karen was putting Lucy away as we arrived. She looked round, but only with the same interest you show a dust-cart or the milkman. She was getting very blasé about our strange activities.

But she managed a small double take—perhaps more a take and a half—when I asked her about the inside of Pasha's rug. She didn't ask why though; she just moved down to his box and threw up a corner of it.

It was grey. We were luckier than that. It was nearly new, quite unworn inside, but half-way along the back seam there was a tiny V-shaped tear in the wool lining. For all the world as if it had been snagged on barbed wire.

While Karen was finding something else for Pasha to wear so that forensics could investigate his nightie—as phlegmatic about this strange request as she had been about the previous ones—I asked her about the big chestnut on which so much of our theory depended. I needed to know if he could have done what the scenario required of him. Obviously he wasn't Gilgamesh, or Sally would have had no interest in getting hold of David's horse. But could he still jump big fences at speed—not only the wire fences, one with its temporary top rail and the other hung with six feet of jute rugging, but two big hedges and a hedge and ditch between the wood and Standings? Harry and I had clambered over and through them in ways that a horse could not have done. Pasha had to jump them for the thing to work.

And there was another problem lying in ambush, which we hadn't yet begun to tackle. Where was Pasha all the time Sally was up at the house? Clearly she hadn't ridden him into the yard and thrown him into a stable; equally, there was no question of a handy groom to hold his reins under the shelter of the high hedge. You might tether a donkey with the reasonable expectation that it would be there on your return, but what about an event horse? Could you teach them to stay, like a collie dog?

With the possible exception of riding horses, there was nothing in the world that Karen liked doing better than talking about them. I could hardly remember now the quiet thing in the background that she had seemed for the last twelve months. I think the reason we got on so well, the difference in our ages and experiences notwithstanding, was that I was a new audience for her fund of horse talk.

At my question, her face brightened and her voice warmed.

"Pasha? He's a real gentleman. I'd never had much to do with him until this week, but he really is a super horse. He's the sort of horse you'd pick for yourself—well, I would. He mightn't make winning times in big competitions now, but he'd never let you down either. Whatever he's got, he gives you. You can't not like a horse that genuine. There aren't that many of them about."

"How high would he be able to jump now?"

She shrugged. "It's a bit hard to say. He'll have jumped in competitions where the maximum height was three feet eleven; but to clear that much solid timber from sloping ground, say, or at an angle, he might have to jump five feet."

I pictured it and whistled softly. Five feet was me standing in soft ground. It was the gate into the sand school. There was nothing that big between here and Standings.

It left only one problem. "You know how in cowboy films everyone hitches his horse to a rail in front of the saloon, and when they've finished throwing each other through the swinging doors the horses are still there? Can you actually do that?"

Karen looked round at me and grinned. "Course you can. If you've an infinite supply of bridle leather and don't mind chasing your horse down the main street for half a mile before you can ride home."

"Ah. They tend not to co-operate?"

"Well, I don't think ours would. It's just something you wouldn't do. The first thing you learn in this job is that you never tie a horse up by its bridle. You can tie them by a headcollar as long as they're somewhere confined—in a horsebox, say, or the stable—but you always use a quick-release knot and tie them to a loop of twine rather than a fixed ring. Because if they panic, they'll pull back until something breaks, and if nothing else gives, a young horse's neck can. Or the headcollar breaks, and you find yourself trying to catch an hysterical horse with nothing to grab but his mane. This is not a nice experience."

I wasn't having a bundle of fun myself. "So it would be pretty reckless to tie a horse to a tree and leave him there for ten minutes."

"You'd have more luck house-training a goldfish."

I was in deep trouble and clutching for straws. "No exceptions?"

She raised an eyebrow and slapped Pasha's rump through his new rug. "There are no rules about horses that you can't find an exception to. Maybe one: What goes up must come down—and even that doesn't apply to a swollen knee." She turned to face me, and once more I was struck by the maturity that hard work and responsibility had fostered in this young woman. "Clio, what's all this about? Jumping wire, hitching rails—whatever are you trying to prove?"

If it had been my investigation, I'd have told her how far we had got and what we'd got stuck on, and asked for her help. But it wasn't, and it would have been presumptuous, conceivably even dangerous, to reveal all without checking first with Harry. I settled for a compromise.

"I will explain fully later. But I need to know now if this horse of Sally's could be ridden across country, then tied to a hedge and left for ten minutes without him either kicking up a storm or hightailing it for home."

"You do, do you?" She looked at me and at the horse. "Ok, then we'd better find out."

She put a leather headcollar on the big chestnut and led him out of his box. "The headcollar's no problem; he could wear that under his bridle. The rope would stuff in your pocket." We went into the cross-country field. The high hedge that ran up to Foxford Wood was where the brief silhouette I thought was the gunman had disappeared. In the half-light of dusk I could quite easily have overlooked half a ton of horse standing there too.

We found a convenient branch, and Karen looped the rope round it and tied it deftly. "You stay here now." For a moment I thought she meant me, but she was talking to the horse. His big eye was kindly and amused.

We went back to the gate, closed it behind us, and leaned on it. The brick wall of the byre was at our backs, the sand school between us and the house. We could just see the big ginger rump. It didn't appear to be doing very much. Once it swung round quite gently, as if Pasha had grown bored with the game and decided to wander off, but the pressure of the rope brought him up short and he came to rest again. There was a slight ripple of movement that might have been him venting a patient sigh. After ten minutes we went back and found him waiting exactly as we had left him.

"There's always one," said Karen cheerfully. "Any time you go on record with a statement about what horses will or won't do, there's always one ready to make an utter fool of you." She rubbed the inquisitive big nose with no resentment whatever.

There had been, while he had waited by this hedge before, a sudden sharp sound from the house, the crack of a rifle fired from inside the French windows of the study. I clapped my hands sharply to simulate it. Karen jumped out of her skin. The horse flicked his ears forward, recognised the sound as more unaccountable human behaviour, and lipped a bit more hawthorn out of the hedge. He was bombproof, unflappable—the exception that proved the rule.

Karen pulled the rope loose and cast me something of a glare. "What was that good for?"

"About eight years," I said, and led the way back to the gate, trying not to give way to the oddly mingled senses of triumph and sorrow that I felt.

CHAPTER 3

Speed and Endurance

I

That afternoon, when Gilgamesh had completed his show-jumping round, Ellen phoned David in the hospital and David phoned me. Bless him, he sounded as thrilled for his horse as if he'd been able to ride him.

He also sounded a lot stronger than last time I'd spoken to him. "He went clear," he said. "He" for the horse, I noticed, not "she" for the rider. "Even with the penalties for yesterday's run-out, he can't finish below eighth. He might move up a place if someone above him has a cricket-score."

"That's pretty good, isn't it?"

"It's bloody marvellous, in all the circumstances."

"It all comes down to the trainer, of course," I said with a grin I wasn't sure he'd be able to hear.

"Bloody right it does," he replied with a beam that was perfectly audible.

"How are you feeling now?" I hadn't been at the hospital for nearly a week, although at least twice in that time I had told myself I absolutely had to and the housework could wait. The housework had in fact waited, but I still hadn't got down to see David, though the hospital was so close you could see it from the more open parts of The Brink. Time wasn't the problem. The problem was how bad I felt about what had happened that I hadn't been able to prevent, and now about what I knew that I couldn't tell him. He'd have to be told, of course, at some point. It would be like a fresh bullet exploding in his flesh.

For now, thank God, he could hear none of this in my voice, only the question I had asked. "Not bad; not at all bad. I can wiggle my toes now," he added proudly.

I knew: Ellen had called at the cottage all excited on the day the news broke. "That's tremendous, David. Really—you could have been a lot longer with no real motor response. How are you getting on with your physiotherapist?"

Awe and gloom floated down the wire. "She's got a moustache and hands like the shovels on a D7. She's called Sophi. I think she left Greece in disgust when the Colonels turned soft on her." In view of how many men fall in love, however briefly, with their nurses, it's odd how few people like their physiotherapists. Even their colleagues tend not to like physiotherapists.

We chatted a little while longer, about his horses and his physiotherapist and his magnificent ability to wiggle his toes, and about how excruciatingly boring hospital is once you start feeling better. Then somebody come in with his tea and whisked the phone away while we were still shouting goodbyes.

I was glad of his news, but more than that, I was glad to have heard from him, glad of the growing strength in his voice, the way he was beginning to relate to things beyond the end of his toes. Ellen had been right: whatever kind of a recovery he made, whether he was left with some disability, or none, or confined to a wheelchair for the rest of his days, David Aston lacked aptitude as a cripple. The worst he'd ever be was a man who couldn't move round too well.

And I can only assume that it was this sense of good cheer that came from talking to him which blinded me to the absolute certainty that after Ellen had phoned David with the news from Bramham, Sally would phone her dad.

Which of course was why, when Ellen drove the horsebox into the yard at Foxford at two o'clock the next afternoon to find herself met by Harry and three other police, one of them a WPC, she was alone in the cab with no one to share her amazement.

I was there because of the effect that Sally's arrest was bound to have on Ellen; Harry wanted someone to stay with her when he took away the woman who had shot her husband. In the event, we were all pretty shaken and comforting one another.

Before the box had come to a halt Harry was up on the running board peering through the open window. "Ellen, where's Sally?"

"She's coming on later. Harry, what's all this about?" Fear supplanted surprise in her face. "David? . . ."

"Is fine," Harry interjected quickly. "Really. It's not you we were waiting for; it's Sally. Where is she?"

"I told you. She's coming down later with some people she met. Harry, whatever is the matter?"

Harry took her inside and told her. I gave Karen a hand unloading Gilgamesh—my main contribution was standing on one side of the ramp with the yard brush—then I followed them indoors.

They were in the kitchen and Harry already had the kettle on. I sat down beside Ellen and took her hand over the scrubbed pine table. "It's a bastard, isn't it?"

Shock had knocked the bottom out of her eyes and her voice. "I don't believe it." She didn't mean that, of course; she meant she didn't want to believe it, but the difference wasn't significant.

I nodded. "We could always be wrong."

She really didn't believe that. "No," she said slowly. "It fits—doesn't it?"

"We think so."

Harry said, "These people she said she'd come home with—when did she decide?"

"Last night. There was a party after the prize-giving. We thought we'd stay the night rather than drive through it. Midway through the evening she came over and said she'd met these people from near Coventry who had a horse they'd like her to ride for them. She said she was going back with them today; she'd give it a try and see if she was interested. She said—" Ellen's voice caught and she started again, carefully. "She said she'd need a class horse for when David wanted his back.

"She helped me load the box this morning and that was the last I saw of her. I thought it was a little odd—it's a long way to travel a horse on your own—but damn it, she's not a groom. I thought she was helping us out of the goodness of her heart, and I wasn't about to complain if she wanted to do something about her own future as well. God damn it, Clio"—a rare outburst, this, from a woman who seldom swore—"what would you have done?"

"Exactly the same." I meant it. "What else could you do?"

"So the last time you saw her," said Harry, "was—what time this morning?"

"About eight-thirty. I was on the road before nine."

"A shade over five hours then." He sucked his lip. "She could travel a long way in five hours if she knew she had to. Blast Fane— he must have warned her."

"Of course he warned her," I said. "Anyone would. You included."

He didn't answer that, just scowled at me. "Right, I'm going over there."

"I'll stay here."

He returned forty minutes later even angrier than he had left— with Sally, with her father, mostly with himself. His face was set in hard, square lines and chequered with contrasting blocks of red and white. "She's been there. At Standings, just a couple of hours ago. While we were here, watching down the road for the horse-box, she was over at Standings quietly packing a suitcase and filling her pockets with cash. She must have got a ride in something rather faster than a horsebox—not all that difficult, I suppose. Damn and blast! I should have anticipated that. At least I should have guarded against it."

"Did you see the Colonel?"

"Oh yes. Poor bloody man's absolutely shattered, of course. After he'd talked to her on the phone yesterday, he thought she was coming home to clear the mess up, convince us we'd gone off half-cocked again. He still really believed that when she walked in through the front door—that it was some dreadful misunderstanding, that the police had picked up the wrong end of the stick, and stupidity and circumstance had conspired to make a case against her. He didn't still think so when she left half an hour later with her passport and all the cash and valuables she could carry. But he still didn't call us, damn him."

Of course he didn't. How could he? "So what did you do— charge him with being an accessory after the fact?"

He glowered at me. "Don't be bloody silly."

I understood his frustration. An hour ago a radio message to police cars in and around Skipley and on the motorway would have resulted in her arrest. Now that she had had time to change her car and get outside the immediate area of the West Midlands, she would be very much harder to find. I said, "You couldn't have known."

His lip wrinkled, baring his teeth. "I didn't have to know. I should have guessed. It's my job. I should have covered the possibility. Damn it, I could have had her picked up at Bramham yesterday, but I thought it could wait. Three out of ten for judgement, Marsh."

He stood at the kitchen window, looking out on the empty yard. He had taken his cohorts with him to Standings, but he had not brought them back. They were probably on their way down to Skipley, returning to more profitable labours like finding lost dogs and confiscating catapults, and thanking their lucky stars that it hadn't been their decision to make and their heads on the platter.

But it wasn't the first mistake he had made, it almost certainly wouldn't be the last, and he'd live it down, even if Sally Fane remained at large. All the same, the repercussions would be milder if he had her in custody before the chief constable got wind of it.

"Listen, I'd better get back to the station. We're alerting ferries and airports; I've got a picture of her to put on the wire. It's my bet she'll head for Ireland: everyone in the horse world has friends in Ireland. But a fair number of them have friends with boats and light planes too, so just how much chance we have of picking her up I don't know. Still, we'll start getting feedback soon and questions like Does she have a wooden leg? and Could she be travelling as a plate-spinner with an Italian circus? and if I'm not there to field them the cause of interforce relations could be set back ten years. I don't know if I'll be home tonight, or indeed at all."

I went back to Ellen. It seemed to me this latest revelation had knocked the feet from under her as nothing had since David was shot. It wasn't surprising. For three weeks she had counted Sally among her closest friends. She had counted herself fortunate to have the friendship of someone who could offer so much help. They had lived under the same roof, shared meals and chores and late-night television, and Ellen had thought herself deeply in Sally Fane's debt. After the second shooting, she had lived in fear that what had happened to David would also overtake the girl who had offered to take his place, and of the guilt and remorse she would feel then. Learning how much of this had been an illusion and how carefully and deliberately it had been created had come as a real shock.

After quite a long time and quite a lot of coffee she looked up. "How did she do it?" Not why: why would take even longer to come to terms with and probably more than coffee.

So I explained as best I could. "She left it as long as she could and still hope to get the selection. If David had laid himself up without help, she'd have offered her services in the same way; if the horse had knocked himself or lost form, that would have been the end of it anyhow. But with them both still on course for the team, she decided to take matters in hand.

"She was lucky too. She counted on you being home around ten —you don't go out much in the evenings, do you?—but she didn't know you were entertaining. She expected to find David working in his study with the window open. That's what she needed and what he usually did, and because of Mrs. Cooper's phone call, that's how it worked out. If Mrs. Cooper hadn't phoned just then or if Harry had been home in time for dinner, I don't know what she'd have done. Probably gone home and tried again another night.

"She had it all planned when she invited the Parkers and the Maudsleys to dinner. She left Pasha tacked up in his stable, with a headcollar under his bridle and a change of clothes and a parka waiting ready for her. Earlier in the day she went up to Foxford Wood and draped a jute rug over the wire fence. She nailed a plank over the wire into your field; she may have done that some time before.

"She arranged for dinner to be over just before ten so she'd be serving coffee as the sun was going down. After she spilt the stuff over herself, everyone there thought she was upstairs changing; but she changed in the stable and was already galloping up the fields to the wood when Colonel Fane's news came on. She jumped through the wood, turned along the hedge here, and stopped somewhere short of the gate. She tied Pasha to a branch and left him there. We couldn't see him from the house—the angle's wrong —and it was a bit late for anybody to be wandering about the fields. If anyone had seen him, they'd assume he was one of yours anyway.

"We don't know yet where she got the gun. But she arrived here with it slung on her back, so it didn't interfere with her riding, and she worked herself round the front of the house to the study window. She must have passed under the drawing-room window while we were in there, waiting for David to finish with Mrs. Cooper. I suppose the drop from the terrace would give all the cover she needed.

"David had his back to the window. She walked close up behind him without him hearing her and put a bullet into him. She's a good shot apparently. I think she placed that bullet quite carefully to end his chance of selection without ending his life or even his career. If she'd intended to kill him or hadn't cared whether she killed him or not, she'd have been much safer shooting from further away."

What else? Oh yes, the painting. "The picture was supposed to be the motive, but she couldn't risk being caught with it. She took it off the wall and immediately tried to dispose of it. She took the cover off the slurry tank in the yard—that was the sound we heard —but she had some trouble fitting it through. That's why she was still there when I came outside to watch for the ambulance. I saw her hurrying towards the hedge; then I lost sight of her in the dusk.

"She must have seen me too. When she saw me looking at the hatch later, she ran the horse at me to take my mind off it. When I went back again, she tried to kill me. This time I was lucky. If she hadn't heard Harry's car coming, I'd be dead."

"But—who shot at her?" Ellen's voice was tiny, her face perplexed. Neither of us was saying Sally's name as if doing so might conjure her up. It conveyed a subtle impression of awe, if not actual reverence.

"No one did." I outlined the quite simple means by which she had managed this vitally convincing deception, and rather reluctantly added the information that it was Harry, not I, who worked it out.

"Will they get her?"

"I imagine so. Perhaps not right away." But it's difficult enough for someone to disappear for long out of a modern, computerized society when her name and appearance are known to the authorities seeking her. Hightailing it to the Colonies and going native isn't a reliable means of vanishing in a world dominated by communications. Anyway, it's hard to travel far without proving who you are. It's hard to get work or somewhere to live. She might go down and stay down for months, but then she'd come up again and someone would notice. And Harry would hear.

"It's so strange," said Ellen, shuddering. "I can't get used to the game having changed ends. I keep starting a thought on the basis that she's a friend who's helping us out and then having to stop and change it all round because it's not true; what happened to us was not only her doing but her choice, quite deliberate and calculating. I still don't understand it. Is she mad?"

It was a serious question, not invective, and I tried to answer it. "No. Not what you and I mean by mad. She's entirely rational—supremely so: she damn near outthought the lot of us. She knows that what she did was both illegal and wrong; she knew that when she was doing it. There was nothing of the sudden brainstorm about it.

"At the same time, it's not normal behaviour—not even normal criminal behaviour. I'm not a psychiatrist, you understand, and never was, but I think the word to describe her ability to plot and carry out those actions over a protracted period of time, apparently unhindered by guilt or any sensitivity over the consequences for anyone but herself, is psychopathy. It's a disorder of the character rather than the mind; essentially, the psychopath can't make peace with society. The psychopath who wants something blames the rest of us for the fact that he hasn't got it and so anything he has to do to get it is, in his own mind, justified. We asked for it; it's all our fault anyway."

Ellen stood up abruptly, hugged her arms round herself, gave me a kind of twitchy grin. "Any time now I'm going to start feeling sorry for her."

I smiled back with admiration and affection. "I don't know whether she deserves your sympathy. I know she wouldn't value it. But it's the fact that you can feel that way that's the difference between you and her. The only one she can feel for is her. That's a pretty crippling condition."

Ellen nodded, and looked away and round the cornices of the room. There was nothing to see up there; it just kept the tears in her eyes from spilling out. After a minute she cleared her throat. "Speaking of which, will you give me one more straight answer to a direct question?"

"If I can."

"Is there any chance of David being fit to ride in the World Championships?"

It could have been a harder question. This one I could answer without much difficulty and without much prospect of being wrong. "No. Not this year." It wasn't professional, but it was true.

"Right," she said briskly, rounding on me with something like relief. "Then I know what to do about the horses. First thing tomorrow they go down the fields, and they're not coming up again until David brings them up."

"And Gilgamesh?"

"Gilgamesh especially. I'm not sending him anywhere she can follow. By the time he's been at grass for a week he won't be fit enough to compete again until after the team has been picked. The big bay bastard's been the cause of chaos enough for one year. Now he's going on his holidays."

And with due ceremony the next morning we led the four horses to the big field under the wood and let them go, and watched for fifteen minutes while they galloped round in an ecstasy of excitement, stamping at the ground and kicking at the sun, their heads high, their manes streaming in the storm of their passage. And we thought it was over.

II

The days passed and turned first into weeks and then into the full lazy months of high summer, heady with the scent of flowers and the sound of bees. The horses grew fat and complacent in the field beyond our fuchsia hedge.

The story of what had been happening up on The Brink got out and dominated Skipley gossip for perhaps a fortnight. Then a local minister was seduced in his own organ-loft by a senior choirboy, and the names Aston and Fane dropped out of currency between one meeting of the Mothers' Union and the next.

Speculation continued a little longer in the eventing world, though I only heard it second-hand now through Karen. But it was whispered, half-ashamed speculation, as if the fancy knew that in some measure its own hearty ruthlessness, its time-honoured tradition of competitors coming back with their back-protectors or on them, had played a part in the tragedy that had overtaken two of its good young riders. And soon that too died away, as the focus of interest shifted from those who would not be at the World Championships to those who would.

The police search for Sally Fane was not (as they would tell you themselves) called off. But demands on police time are high. Newer crimes supervened, and when the initial wave of enquiries proved fruitless, subsequent waves were less impressive, the pressure diminished as manpower was syphoned off to tackle other crimes. What was for ten days a national issue reverted, after perhaps another month, to being a Skipley CID problem again.

Slowly and steadily through the summer weeks David's recovery progressed. As his wound healed, so the communications network that was his central nervous system, shocked into a temporary close-down, began to consider the resumption of normal services. First sensation and then motor function began to spread, tentatively in the beginning but with increasing confidence as time went on. By the end of June he had taken command of a wheelchair, which broadened his social horizons considerably, and was coming home most weekends. By the end of July he had sufficient use of his legs to move about on crutches for short periods that could only get longer as practice and the appalling Sophi built up the strength he had lost through immobility. After three months, though the fine detail of his future remained beyond resolution, the overall picture was frankly encouraging.

Shock, grief, and shame had struck Colonel Fane at the roots of his existence. He was a proud and honourable man, probably the only man in England less likely than Harry to fiddle his income tax, and his only child was being sought by the police for offences of premeditated mayhem. The strain seemed to sap him like a physical illness, emaciating the narrow-boned face and turning the scrubbed skin to parchment. He was a man in his sixties; after Sally's disappearance he began to look and act like an old man. He hardly left Standings now, and though both Ellen and I made a point of calling on him, he was not at home to me and received

Ellen with such obvious discomfort that she excused herself as soon as she decently could and did not go again.

Harry went through a period of slightly strained relations with his chief constable over the fact that Sally had been emptying her drawers at home while the dragnet waited for her at Foxford. The rather snide side-swipes which Harry bore stoically for the first fortnight and with increasing irritation for the next stopped abruptly on the night that two mounted constables and another four on foot were totally submerged under a running battle between National Front and CND supporters after a rally which the chief constable predicted almost no one would turn up for.

Then one afternoon in August the phone rang. I was working in the garden, at rather less than full steam ahead because of the sun beating on my back and the drowsy murmurings in the fuchsia hedge and the soporific smell of honeysuckle and roses. I considered letting it ring, but Harry had been hoping to finish early and go over to Stratford if he could get tickets for the Royal Shakespeare and book a meal somewhere, so it was likely to be him calling to cancel or confirm. I struggled out of the hammock—it's a hard life, being a writer—and stumbled inside.

"Clio? It's Ellen." That quickly I could hear the slightly odd note in her voice, a suppressed excitement. "Listen, something's happened. Can you come over? I've got something to show you."

She refused to be drawn, so after a moment, a shade reluctantly, I said I'd be up in ten minutes. "I'll meet you at the stables," she said.

I wasn't really dressed for visiting, even for visiting Ellen. To be honest, I was hardly dressed at all. After a moment's consideration I pulled a shirt over my singlet, belted it over my shorts, and pushed my bare feet into moccasins. Thus sanitised for public consumption, and leaving a note in case Harry got in within the next half-hour, I pulled the cottage door behind me and padded into the lane. I could have driven—the car was sitting there—but it was a hot day and I thought I could cope with the walk easier than with the petrol fumes. That was a mistake.

Ellen's big car, which David had already tried driving on one of his weekends home (witness the small dent in the offside wing and the larger one in the box hedge), was not in its usual place under the coach-arch. I thought she might have driven it into the stable yard for some reason connected with her surprise, so I wandered on down there, looking for her.

The car wasn't in the yard, but one of the stable doors was open. To the best of my knowledge, those stables hadn't been occupied for ten weeks.

"Ellen?" I stuck my head inside, but there was nothing and nobody there. I walked back up the alley towards the house. "Ellen!" The kitchen door and the big main door under the portico were both locked. I walked round the terrace, tapping windows, but clearly there was no one at home.

It really was most odd. All I could think was that in the few minutes since she called me something had happened to take Ellen out of the house in a rush; and since she hadn't thought to leave me a note, it must have been something urgent and important. I immediately thought of David and wondered if she could have had a message from the hospital. I decided that when I got home, I'd phone the hospital and make sure everything was all right.

I heard a sound then, a dull sound that was stilled before I had time to work out what it was or where it came from. It might have come from the far side of the byre; I was back in the stable yard now. It could almost have been the hatch-cover of the slurry tank. "Ellen, are you there?"

Long seconds passed, so many I was beginning to think I'd imagined it; there was no one there and all I had heard was the wind in the loose and rusted gutterings. But there was no wind, not even breeze enough to lift the dust lying in the empty yard. I looked up the yard, in the direction of the sound, but all I could see was the brick byre that was almost as old as the house. David's father, who took his farming more seriously than his son did, had excavated the slurry tank and installed the slatted floor. It was the latest thing in cattle husbandry when it was done. All it was used for now was housing a small beef herd for fattening over the winter. Of course, if David had to give up riding, it might yet fulfil the purpose for which it was designed.

Then I heard it again, a dull ringing like someone chopping wood heard through an acre or two of dense timber, a soft, slow, hollow, rhythmic percussion. It was a sound I had never heard before, but I recognised it almost at once. It was a sound which had no business here, at this time and in these circumstances, with no one at the house and no one but me in the yard.

It was the sound of a horse, its heavy hooves unshod, pacing a slow and measured tread on the concrete surface of the yard, out of sight behind the byre. Its stride was so slow, so deliberate, that I could hear each individual footfall, like the beat of a muffled drum.

I cannot explain the deep unease which grew in me with every throb of that drum. It was an unexpected sound, with Foxford apparently deserted and the horses ostensibly out to grass, but not so very unlikely. If the field gate had been sprung by too energetic a tail-scrubbing, the culprit might have wandered up through the sand school and up the far side of the byre, where Gilgamesh and I had our close encounter that seemed then so violently unpredictable and was anything but.

But I knew, without knowing how, that nothing so mundane as a weak gate explained that measured footfall out of sight. Unease deepened towards fear. I think it was the very slowness of the beat which struck such chill into my heart. It was unnatural. No normal animal would walk so slowly on concrete, where there wasn't even a blade of grass to pick at in passing. It was the tenor of a hunter stalking prey. It was the stuff of nightmare.

I didn't know what to do. There was nothing immediately threatening about the thing, yet I felt threatened. I could see nothing, but I wanted to hide. The slow, slow stride made me want to run like hell. I cast indecisive glances back and forth. I could shut myself in a stable, where I would be safe enough if it was a loose horse but trapped if it was not. I could run up my side of the byre while it walked slowly up the other, and cross the upper yard behind the house like an Olympic sprinter in the hope of reaching the drive before it reached me. If it was a horse, of course, I couldn't outrun it. But if it was a horse, why would it want to chase me?

The note of the hoofbeats changed as it reached the far corner of the byre. As near as damn it, it was already between me and the drive: if it had ever been an avenue of escape, it was cut off now. I stood, undecided still in the middle of the stable yard, and listened to the slow drumming of hooves and the fast drumming of my heart, and the indescribable but quite distinctive sound of my blood turning to water. And still nothing at all had happened, except that I'd heard a horse walking past the byre and responded with a panic attack that even in the middle of it I could not explain or justify.

Behind the bottom stables rose the original barnyard wall, eight feet of grimed and weathered brick. The sparse end of Foxford Wood ran into a kind of rough heath and died against it like a high tide running out of energy and dying with a hiss against a sea-wall. If there had been a way over that wall—a way suitable for a short, middle-aged woman writer rather than a six-foot, twenty-five-year-old paratrooper—I would have taken it and circled back home through the lanes before whatever was stalking me found a way to follow. But I could see no prospect of scaling it. There was no ladder in the yard, not even an oil drum or water butt to give me a fighting chance. I was trapped in that yard like a rat in a cage, like a moth in a killing-bottle.

Finally I did the only thing that with dignity I could: I moved to meet the object of my irrational, prophetic fear. I made myself walk from the middle of the yard to the corner so that I could see up the alley towards the house. I don't know that I managed any great show of courage or confidence; I seem to remember taking a long time to cross those few feet, and stopping a number of times, and actually stepping backwards twice. But if the object was that I reach the corner of the stables before the deliberate horse rounded the corner of the byre, then I achieved it. It had cost me blood, but repaid me in some measure by the tiny fillip it gave my self-esteem.

There was time—it seemed plenty of time—for two or three more beats of the hidden drum; then it reached the last corner remaining between us and marched ponderously into my line of vision. It was, of course, a horse, and moreover a horse that I knew: the high head, the imperious eye, the rich brown hide darkling into black. It was Gilgamesh: *the* horse, the horse all our hopes and fears had revolved around since early spring.

And in the half-second or so after the dark, arrogant head emerged from behind the byre and before the rest of the dark muscled body followed suit, I guessed what Ellen's surprise was. It was David—not only home but riding, astride his own great horse for the first time in three and a half months. I would never know what difficulty he had found in getting up there, what pain and exhaustion he had conquered, what weak and uncooperative limbs he had to control. But now he was on top he held the big impatient animal to that measured pace with only a rope halter round his head. In his own way, the horse must have been glad to have him back.

And Ellen! One day soon I would murder her for the minute's terror she had put me through. Or perhaps it was unreasonable to credit normal people with the sort of imagination which makes someone a writer of thrillers or a nervous wreck, or both.

I stepped forward with surging relief and a very genuine happiness. "David? Hey, let's have a look at you up there—"

The words died on my lips. The horse stepped out of the wall's eclipse and turned towards me, pivoting as precisely as a well-drilled platoon. Stripped of the customary tack, with only the rope for guidance, he looked bigger than ever, and stronger and, despite the restraint of his stride, more violent. He looked vast and primitive, some ancient Nemesis sent for my undoing.

Which is exactly, give or take the aforementioned imagination, what he was. Because it wasn't David Aston balanced on his broad, muscular back, long legs dangling loosely down the burnished flanks. It was Sally Fane.

III

The last time I had seen her was in the fullness of her triumph at Bramham. She looked very different now. Instead of riding clothes, she wore jeans, a shirt that had gone too long without sight of an iron, and no hat. Her hair was longer and wilder than I remembered, a tangle of curls rioting round the drawn framework of her face. Her face was thin, sallowed as if with too little sun, and set in iron-hard lines. Her eyes looked down at me from under half-lowered lids, and there was fire and ice and implacable hatred in their depths.

Ellen hadn't called me. Sally had.

I didn't know what to say. I didn't know why she was here, and I wasn't sure I wanted to. I didn't know what she was doing on David's horse or why she had summoned me here when Ellen was clearly out.

Finally I managed, "They've been looking for you." There was a tremor in my voice. It would have been remarkable if there had not been: my insides were shaking like blancmange. Like a blancmange left to set on the foredeck of a three-masted schooner caught in an incipient hurricane off the Azores.

"I know," she said. Her voice was low, heavy but not with any particular meaning. It was impossible yet to judge her intent. Except that she didn't intend me to leave. She had brought the big horse to a standstill in the narrow alley between the stables and the byre. It might have been six feet wide. There was room to push past the horse, but only if she let me. If she turned him sideways, the space would close, and a body could get severely kicked trying to open it up again.

I glanced round me, trying to look less anxious than I felt, but there was nowhere to go, nowhere to retreat except the stables.

There was a door into the byre on this side, but it was never used: the padlock had rusted in the chain holding it shut.

I said, "Where have you been?" If she didn't already know she had me trapped, she wasn't going to learn it from me.

"Here and there." It wasn't meant to be an answer, only a return of serve. She knew she had me all right. She had planned it this way. Another of her careful, well-constructed little plans. Whatever was coming next, she was going to enjoy it.

I said, a little too brightly, "David's a lot better now. He's walking—just a little and on crutches, but walking. He's going to make a pretty good recovery."

"Fine," she said negligently. She couldn't have cared less.

I was in no position to issue threats, but her attitude nettled me. "So it would be pretty bloody silly," I said with some asperity, "to do something now that would get you in more trouble with the law. Wouldn't it?"

She smiled slowly, a smile of pure malice, a psychopath's smile if ever I saw one. Premonition shook me to my soles. "Are you afraid of me?" she asked.

There was no room for manoeuvre. It was a straight choice between telling the truth and lying. So I lied. "No."

The smile went impish round the corners. Few things are more chilling than coyness in the violently insane. Because no matter what I had told Ellen, it was insanity to come back now, to turn her hand to what I could only presume was revenge, when she should have been half a continent away and still running or else talking to the best lawyer she could afford. It was crazy to be here, sitting on the horse of the man she had shot, in his own back yard, plotting revenge against the wife of the senior detective in the case and coyly smiling.

"Oh yes you are," she said, "You're sweating. I can see you sweating. It's a hot day, but not that hot. You're not bothered by my horse, are you?"

"Gilgamesh is not your horse."

I suppose I could have sketched a rough target on my shirt,

front and back, with the legend "Please shoot here," but reminding Sally Fane that the big bay bastard was not her horse but
David Aston's was a reasonable alternative. I saw the smile die on
her lips. Her negligent, indolent gaze hardened again. The iron
rang in her voice.

"Every way that matters he's my horse. I bred him—chose the
stallion for our old mare Venus, who had a lot of decent foals in
her but only one great one. I was with her the night he was born. I
taught him everything from haltering to half-pass."

"And then you sold him to David."

"I did not sell him!" It was as if I'd accused her of selling a
baby. Plain anger and something like grief supplanted the spite in
her voice. The four-year-old wound still ached. "My dad sold him.
He made me choose—between him and Pasha. He wouldn't foot
the bills for both of them. And Pasha was winning for me then,
and Gilgamesh was only promising to. All he needed was a bit of
time to come right, but the old sod wouldn't give me any. So I kept
Pasha. You need a horse on the day in this game. A nearly horse
can't take you the places you have to be."

"All right, it was a tough break. But David only bought the
horse, he didn't make you sell him."

"He knew what that horse meant to me! He knew I wanted to
ride him. I was glad enough when David took him. I thought—"
She stopped abruptly, the sentence unfinished.

So Harry's shot in the dark had been close enough. "You
thought you'd be coming to Foxford with him."

"No!" I think she was a little shocked at how much she'd given
away in her anger. "I mean, there was never anything official—an
engagement, anything like that. It was just— Well, both our fa-
thers wanted it. I thought David wanted it: he was always up at
our place or dragging me over here. I just kind of assumed that
sometime we'd probably do something about it."

"You didn't so much sell the horse as lend-lease him."

But instead David had married Ellen and kicked Sally's expec-
tations out from under her. She might have forgiven him that and

settled for friendship and a future like more of the past if he hadn't kept her horse. That hadn't been the deal she agreed to. The arrangement existed only in her head, but she held David guilty of breaking it. The World Championships had been why she acted as she did this season rather than next, but the tragedy had been stalking him, waiting for a time and a place to happen. She was always going to reclaim her horse and pay David back for welching on the contract with her that he didn't know he'd entered into.

Now she was back, and standing between me and safety. I believed she could do anything to someone she blamed for her difficulties, and do it, moreover, without any compunction.

I took a deep breath and said reasonably, "Sally, I'll have to go now; Harry's waiting for me." I think I kept the fear out of my voice.

"Superintendent Harry bloody Marsh," she spat with an access of hatred that surprised me even after what had gone before, "is behind his bloody little desk in his bloody little office and has no idea that his bloody little wife is trying to talk her way out of a tight spot with a homicidal maniac."

I said, "You're not a maniac, Sally," with as much quiet confidence as I could muster.

"No," she agreed. Her voice had dropped back to a tone of near normality, but there was still a glitter in her eye. "I am homicidal though."

She nudged the horse towards me. The broad chest in its gleaming conker-coloured hide came at me a step at a time, filling my sight like a wall. The long face, with its lofty, imperious eyes, hung over my head like a sentence, the warm breath stirring my hair. The vast, hard hooves were inches from my moccasins. I stepped back. And again and again.

I moved cautiously to one side. If I could see past the horse, perhaps I could run past him. He would hardly get turned in the narrow alley between the buildings; Sally would have to ride him into the lower yard and turn there. If it gave me only a few seconds' head start, it might be enough to find a refuge where he could not follow. I had no wish to meet Sally Fane, young and strong and unbalanced, in any kind of combat, but if the choice was between that and facing up to her on the horse, it was no contest.

But she saw my purpose and the great, quiet, dangerous horse shadowed me, pushing me down the alley with his shoulder. The precision and delicacy with which his rider controlled his movements was remarkable but, to me at that time, something less than a delight. I had to get past him, because if Sally wanted me in the lower yard, it had to be in my interests to avoid going there. But my options were limited. The horse was too big to shoulder aside. I might conceivably dodge from his front to his rear end so quickly that he couldn't follow, but then I'd have to squeeze between the wall and his lightning heels. John Wayne might have tried diving under his belly, and if the Duke could fit, then certainly I could. But Warner Brothers horses were probably more used to such liberties and less likely to dance the Duke to a bloody pulp than Gilgamesh was if I tried it.

I had to do something, and I had to do it before the fear that was rising inside me flooded over, gumming up my working parts and rendering me incapable of any action. I spun a mental coin and it came up tails, so I tried it. I feinted to one side, and as the head and shoulders swung to close the gap, I lurched the other way to race up the flank and past the rear end and up the yard and past the house and God knows where after that.

I hadn't realised she had the same sort of control over the horse's quarters as she had over his front. Instead of following my move with his head, Gilgamesh kept turning away from me, so that his rump moved over to the wall, closing the gap like a cork in a bottle. I couldn't adjust to this new situation quickly enough; I ran into the powerful haunch while it was still turning, and the force locked up in that smooth muscularity not only stopped me in my tracks but slammed me back down the alley like a first service from Ivan Lendl.

I lost my footing and rolled in the dust. When I worked out

which way was up and followed it with my eyes, I found the big, dark bulk standing over me and Sally Fane watching me with something akin to pleasure.

I spat the stable taste out of my mouth and climbed to my feet, watching her in return. My breath was coming fast—I could hear it in my sinuses like a tube train whistling through Green Park—but a tiny, detached part of me noted with interest and approval that resentment was fueling the adrenalin supply and the fear was turning at least partially to anger. I was forty-one years old, a married woman, and a professional in two disciplines, and absolutely nobody had the right to roll me in the dirt like a grubby schoolboy!

Except to me, it hardly mattered what I said. But I wanted her to know that if terror was what she craved, she'd have to get her satisfaction elsewhere. I was no longer afraid of her in that way. I was not, of course, unaware of what she and this brute of a horse could do to me, but that was different. Fearing what an enemy may do is only human; it's fearing the enemy which paves the road to cowardice. I didn't want to be hurt, but even less did I want to feel myself a coward before her.

I said gruffly, "Make the most of it. Where you're going the only horses wear uniform, blow whistles at slopping-out time, and you address them as Ma'am." As an assessment of the British penal system in the 1980s, perhaps it lacked sophistication, but it worked for me.

Sally seemed undismayed. I had expected her to strike at me or run me down, but she only smiled quite gently, as if I were a dim child who had once again confused the functions of its mouth and its ear when faced with a spoonful of porridge. "Prison? Oh, I'm not going to prison, Clio," she said, as if that was that.

"You think you'll get a secure hospital? Well, try for it by all means, though I imagine the security's much the same and the food worse. Maybe the horses wear white starched caps, but any way you look at it, Sally, you have a great future behind you."

"Nobody's locking me up. I'd rather be dead."

"Yes, OK."

She laughed aloud at that, a rich peal of laughter that momentarily filled the yard, echoing between the byre and the stables and the brick back wall. Then the good humour drained out of her as swiftly and completely as if a plug had been pulled. Her eyes hardened and grew cold, her gaze snapping like icicles. The planes of her face set firm, the bone structure prominent beneath. Her voice dropped again to that low, husky register, charged with portent, but now the ambivalence was gone. She made no effort to disguise the hatred she bore me because her clever, comprehensive deception had failed. It showed in the stern, inhuman lines of her face and body, powerful and personal.

Maybe she overestimated my role in her downfall, but not by all that much. I had done my best to discover the identity of David's assailant and to prove what she had done and how she had done it. If it was true that I couldn't have completed the chain without Harry's help, it was equally the case that he might not have begun it without mine. I was in a large measure responsible for Sally's situation. My own notwithstanding, I could still find it in me to be proud of that.

Fury reverberated in her voice. "Do you think I don't know? Why you did it—the whole damn pack of you, you and Harry and David and my dad—do you think I don't know? You're jealous of me, jealous of what I can do. You couldn't rest, any of you, until you'd spoiled it for me.

"Other people get the support of their families and friends, but not me: my dad sells my horse from under me, and my best friend buys him to keep me from beating him. Hell, I don't know why I expected any different. I've never had anything in my life that I haven't worked my guts out for.

"One good season," she said, the words running out of her like a river in spate, like a bitter tide. "That was all I needed: one good season four years ago, and it would have been me the selectors were after anyway. You'd think my dad could have given me that. You'd think David could have done that much for me: it didn't have to come to him or me; he could have helped me without being made to. And you! All you had to do was stay out of it. Everything would have worked out, except for you. With Gilgamesh I'd have made the team, and after that, I'd never have been short of a good horse again. You couldn't bear that, could you—you petty, jealous, little people!"

Listening to her, knowing nothing about the background, you could have believed her. You could have heard in the grief and the anger of her voice the authentic ring of martyrdom and believed that, for reasons best known to ourselves, her father and her neighbours had conspired at her downfall. It was undoubtedly how she saw it, which was itself graphic testimony to the disturbance of her mind and emotions. She was not only irrational; she was almost beyond reach of reason.

Her voice sank back to a chilly whisper and her eyes crackled with ice. "I'm going to make you sorry you ever got involved. I'm going to make you sorry you came here."

My heart sank too. The posturing was over, the fencing and feinting, the game of cat and mouse. She was ready to do what she had come back for. "I'm going to make you sorry you ever heard of Foxford, or David Aston, or sweet, silly Ellen. I'm going to make you sorry—"

"Don't tell me," I said. I don't know where that note of gruff, sardonic humour came from, but I was glad to hear it. "You're going to make me sorry I was ever born." But even as I said it, I knew I was spitting in the wind. The threat might lack originality, but that didn't mean she couldn't carry it out. Clichés get to be clichés by conveying some very specific meaning very accurately. I'd seen enough suffering in my time to know just how powerfully one could crave non-existence.

"Do you think it's a joke? You have shattered my dreams and ruined my future, and you think it's a joke? Damn you!" she cried, and all the emotion, all the hatred and rage and frustration banked up behind the wall of ice and words finally broke through. The force of it shook her shoulders where she loomed above me. "I had it all worked out! I was so careful. I was even careful not to hurt David more than I had to. If you hadn't interfered, it would all have worked out. After I'd ridden the horse in the World Championships, there'd be no way he could have taken him back, he'd have had to offer me some kind of partnership. It would have been OK, it would have been good—him training and me riding. We'd have been a good team."

"You shot him!"

"It was nobody's business but ours!" I swear she believed it: that there was nothing fundamentally antisocial about wounding with intent between consenting adults in private. "We'd have worked it out if we'd been left to. But you had to stick your oar in, didn't you? You had to get to the bottom of it. I can understand the police—at least they're paid to be a bloody nuisance—but who the hell asked you to stick your nose in? I mean, what is it with you? Two careers aren't enough; you want to be a detective as well?"

"Call me eccentric if you like," I growled, still backing before the advancing horse. We were in the middle of the yard now, with space all round us. Any time I was going to have to try it again, but even as I steeled myself, I knew that the attempt would be futile. I could not move as fast as Gilgamesh. "But I happen to consider a world worth striving for in which people don't cripple old friends for standing between them and something they want."

"Friend?" she spat. "What kind of a friend was he to me? He took my horse!"

"And wouldn't take you." I saw lightning flash in the thunderheads of her eyes, and as I had known she would, she came at me. The great bulk of the horse launched at me from the clap of her heels. But instead of falling back I shot out sideways, escaping the piston hooves by inches and the surging brown shoulder not at all, for I felt the hard concert of bone and muscle through my shirt thrusting me aside. I used its impetus to help me on my way as I fled.

Having them behind me as I ran was almost worse than facing them. I heard the wild hollow clatter as the horse spun round;

then he was thunder on my trail. It took an effort of will almost greater than I was capable of not to look round, to concentrate every physical and intellectual energy on escape.

I managed it, just, though the thunder in my head was even louder than the beat of my own heart and the rush of my breathing, but still it wasn't enough. After a dozen strides of mine, perhaps three of his, Gilgamesh ran me down like a train and the world slipped beyond my grasp or ken.

IV

I woke drowning. The shock of the cold water hitting me made me throw out arms and legs that collided bruisingly with the solid walls on both sides. I gasped air through the water I had inhaled in great shuddering gulps that were little different to sobs in either sound or import. I had just enough self-awareness to be sorry about that.

For a moment I thought I couldn't see, and a fast-forward of possibilities—detached retinae, brain damage—ripped through my mind before I realised that the least frightful explanation was also the most likely. While I was unconscious, she had dragged me off the yard into a dark place.

I took time—possibly quite a lot of time; I wasn't yet working at optimum efficiency—to explore the idea and decided that was the way of it: I was huddled in a corner on a hard gritty floor currently awash with the minor flood that had woken me, in a place that was dark but not black, thanks to a short vertical slit of light entering on one side. I was in one of the stables, and the light was squeezing through where the bottom door was not quite closed. The top door was shut fast.

My first thought was that she had sluiced me and left. Actually she had sluiced me and stayed to watch the results. As my eyes learned to focus in the dim stable, they found her standing beside the door, just clear of the slit of light, the black rubber bucket swinging lightly in her hand. It must have been as near as damn it full, and she hadn't so much poured it over me as thrown it at me. I could still feel the echo of its impact like a bruise in my chest and a sharp slap in my face.

When she saw my groping senses had found her, she chuckled softly in the half-dark. "Back in the land of the living, Clio? For the moment, at least."

It was a threat, of course, but I wasn't up to subtlety yet. I grunted with the effort to get a knee under me and rise. My whole body felt it had been trampled by a schoolgirl hockey XI. My head swam and I braced myself with a hand either side of me where the walls made the corner. The tutors at Quick Wit & Ready Repartee would have been proud of me. "Bugger off," I said weakly.

"Don't worry," she said, "I shall. In just a minute now. By the time they find you, I'll be long gone, where that snoopy husband of yours is never going to follow. But before I go, because I know Harry'll want to know and there might be enough of you left to tell him, I'm going to tell you where I've been. You know, all those weeks when policemen were leaping out from behind hoardings on every road from Skipley to the coast? When I was the favourite pin-up at passport control at every port and airport in the land, and the TV news kept showing the same clip of Harry saying, 'Of course, it's only a matter of time'?

"Well I'll tell you, Clio, I was at home. Not the first week. The first week I stayed in Birmingham while Harry and the Keystone Kops crawled over Standings with their magnifying glasses and interrogated my dad in the full glare of the study reading-lamp. But after they'd gone, I slipped home and I've been there ever since, sleeping in my own bed, watching telly, waiting for all the fuss to die down. A couple of times I had to dive for the attic, when one of Harry's little friends came calling, but they never really expected to find me there, so they never really looked. Somebody ought to do something about the sheer lack of imagination in the British police force."

It was probably a valid criticism, but not coming from her.

Establishing the link between Sally Fane and the shooting of David Aston had been a triumph of the imagination.

"Then there was the gun," she said. "Anyone with a jot of imagination would have looked back the crime reports and noticed that a .240 deer rifle was among the items stolen from Standings back in January. I took a little bit of a risk with that, but what the hell, if Harry had by some miracle put two and two together and realised it was my gun, he had a report of it being stolen four months earlier. Nothing it did after that could be pinned at my door."

"Four months. Is that how long you were planning it?"

"About that. Though to be fair, I didn't plan the burglary. I didn't even lie about the gun being stolen. But a couple of days later I found it lying in a ditch—I suppose they must have dropped it; maybe they thought someone was onto them and didn't want to be caught with a gun—and I just never reported that I had it back. Having the rifle in those circumstances made the thing possible. I suppose that was when wishful thinking started hardening into a proper plan."

She was boasting about it. I wasn't wringing it out of her; I wasn't even prompting her. She wanted to talk about it, to tell someone how clever she'd been. She wanted to be appreciated. If she couldn't have public acclaim as a rider, she'd have it as a criminal. But it worried me how much she was talking. She'd delayed her escape because it would be easier after the hue and cry had died down. If she was ready to go now, the last thing she needed was me staggering to the nearest telephone before she had five miles under her belt. She wouldn't be talking like this if there was any danger of that. She didn't intend to leave me in any state to stagger to a phone.

She had lured me here quite deliberately, had clearly thought the implications through. She was talking to me so that I could talk to Harry, but she didn't intend me to talk to him immediately or in the near future. She wanted first to be where he couldn't follow. She had money. A private plane could take her to Ireland,

and from Shannon she could go anywhere in the world. Six hours would do; twelve would do better. She meant me to be incommunicado for several hours at the least.

She had dragged me into a stable. Stable doors fasten on the outside, with fittings capable of containing half a ton of temperamental animal power. I wouldn't break my way out in six hours, or twelve hours either. But I was bound to be found before that. When Ellen came home, I'd hear her car and she'd hear me yelling. If Harry came home first, he'd find my note and follow me up here. It might be an hour or two, but surely no more than that before I set the police on her trail.

If I was in any state to talk.

When she saw I had got there, she smiled. "I wondered what to do about you. I very much wanted to have this chat before I left, but I didn't want to risk it rebounding on me. What I needed was someone to watch over you while I got on my way. I couldn't ask my dad. He's been very strange about the whole business: all the time I've been at home he's been pretending I wasn't. Anyway, I don't want to get him into more trouble. Then I thought of someone who couldn't be held legally responsible, even if he broke every bone in your body; someone who's lost as much by your interference as I have. That's why I brought you here. This is his house."

She stepped back swiftly through the open door and latched it behind her. The darkness in the stable deepened. Even before I heard movement in the adjacent box, I knew what to expect. I just didn't know what it would be like.

When she came back, she opened both upper and lower doors, but any hope of escape was blocked once more by an enormous bulk of brown horse.

Sally was grinning. "I can only tell you two things about Gilgamesh that might help you pass the next few hours more comfortably. One, he doesn't like noise. And two, he doesn't like being shut up in the dark."

And she would, of course, shut us up in the dark together, and as the horse in his fear and anger trampled me, my screams would drive him mad. I felt myself beginning to shake, and it had nothing whatever to do with the baptism I had recently undergone.

I stammered, "Ellen will be back."

"Of course she will," agreed Sally, "but not soon. She's taken David to Clent Hills for a picnic. David thinks it was Ellen's idea and Ellen thinks it was David's; both of them think the message came via a nurse at the hospital. They may be a little confused if they find out differently, but what the hell, they'll be enjoying themselves and they won't hurry back. I doubt if Ellen will be back here much before midnight. She probably won't come down to the yard until Gilgamesh gets hungry enough to shout for food. There's hay in the manger, so he'll be all right until morning.

"Of course, you'll have been missed by then, but there's no reason anyone would look for you here, is there?"

There was, but I was keeping that to myself as if my life depended on it. Quite possibly my life did depend on it. I might go one round, or two, with the big bay bastard, but I wasn't going to go the distance.

Holding the lead rope in one hand, she made a show of checking the watch on her other wrist. "Good grief, is that the time? Amazing how it flies when you're enjoying yourself. Listen, Clio, I'll have to go soon. I have a plane to catch. I'd just like you to know I shall think of you fondly whenever I see a road accident or someone using a pile-driver. I hope you get all you deserve. I hope you go through the rest of your life bent double. My only regret is that I couldn't get your man Harry as well. Being nursemaid to a crippled wife will have to serve for him."

With that, she urged the horse forward, stepping deftly back as he passed her and slamming the two doors in rapid and noisy succession, leaving me in near darkness with a big, dangerous animal whose frustration was filling the stable with the hot breath from his cracking nostrils.

I kept very still. You wouldn't believe how still I kept. I breathed through one nostril at a time. I pushed my body so far into the corner that my backside was in danger of becoming wedge-shaped. I hardly knew I was there myself; I was sure the horse didn't know I was there.

Like hell he didn't know. He knew exactly where I was, and if he didn't know exactly who I was, he knew two things about me: that I wasn't one of his small band of friends and admirers and that I was responsible for him being shut up in this dark and scary stable. No, three things he knew. He could also smell my fear. Damn it, *I* could smell my fear, even using one nostril at a time.

I stayed where I was, very still, waiting for my eyes and his to adjust to the dark and both our nerves to steady. I wondered if I should say anything to him. Sally said he hated noise, but surely a soft and friendly greeting could do nothing but good?

"Easy, boy; there's a good lad," I murmured, soft as butter and friendly as a game-show groupie. My adjusting eyes saw his adjusting eyes flash whitely, his ears clamp flat, and his big rear end swing menacingly in my direction. The clatter of his own hooves on the bare floor sent his head up and down like a nodding Alsatian in the back window of a Renault 5.

The big bay bastard would have you as soon as look at you, Ellen had said. I had hoped she'd exaggerated, but nothing I had seen so far suggested it. I didn't know if Gilgamesh was genuinely capable of the mayhem Sally claimed, but I had to work on the assumption that he was. I could bear to be proved wrong if she was only trying to scare me.

Moving only my eyes. I searched the closed box for some way of improving my lot, if only marginally. Apart from my new authority on the product of their digestive systems, almost all I knew about horses was that one end bit and the other kicked. Since I'd never heard much adverse comment on the middle, I decided that was probably the safest place to be; and since the horse seemed to have settled with his head to the door and his eye pressed to the tiny horizontal slit between upper and lower halves, it seemed a good idea to move from my back corner up the side wall to a point midway between teeth and hooves. I took a deep, soft breath and edged forward.

It was a bad move. I saw the big muscles on the dark rump bunch, the strong, absurdly slender legs stiffen, the neck arch downward; then he took one quick, precise step backward and launched a mighty inch-perfect kick that would have knocked me into the middle of next week if the stable wall hadn't been there to stop me.

Back on the floor in my corner, huddled round the sick hurt in my midriff and fighting for enough breath to cry with, managing only the tears and a sound like whooping cough that threatened to bring him down on me again, I considered stoically the possibility that things could have been worse: the big bay bastard could still have had his iron shoes on. I sniffed in admiration for my own courage, and a mournful tear dripped off the end of my nose.

But the tortured sound of me trying to refill lungs he'd knocked the air out of once didn't provoke a second attack, so in due course I tried again. I waited until I could breathe quietly, until the spastic shaking of my limbs had died back to a gentle tremble, until my muscles had some strength again and my knees had stopped trying to bend both ways. Then I had another go.

He got me twice this time, once with both hooves in the chest and once with one on the point of my shoulder as I went down. His other hoof missed my head by inches, if that. I felt the wind of its passing in my ear.

For a long time, then, I lay in the gutter at the back of the stable, too hurt to move and anyway too scared to try. For the first time I understood what they had meant—Ellen and Sally and Karen, all treating this big, talented, dangerous horse with infinite caution and respect. He really could kill you. For the first time I realised that Sally's threats were to be taken absolutely at face value. If help didn't come soon, he would certainly cripple me. If it didn't come until a romantic sun had set over Clent Hills, it wouldn't matter whether it came or not.

He was back at the door, which meant his back end was pointing my way again. He was drinking in that sliver of light and air as greedily as a man thirsting in a desert drinks water, and every few moments his eye flicked back in its socket to check that I was still where he'd put me. It was a vicious look, right enough, but there was fear there too. He was afraid of this creature crawling round where he couldn't see it in the hateful dark; it was only his nature to react aggressively to things he feared and didn't know.

It was that which made him what he was, a superlative sportsman. When the urge to win is so powerful that it overrides the fierce instincts of pain and self-preservation, it's separated from an urge to kill only by a veneer of civilisation so thin that the light shines through. In Gilgamesh the veneer was torn and everybody knew it. It had also worn through in Sally, but no one had realised until it was too late to avoid a tragedy. Neiher of them was wholly responsible for the monsters they had become.

All of which was interesting in a philosophical way but of no immediate help or comfort to me. I had to find some way of surviving the next minutes and hours. We'd been together like this, Gilgamesh and I in the dark intimacy of his stable, for maybe ten minutes, and already I had his footprints all over me. I had been lucky, to the extent that so far there didn't seem to be anything broken, but you couldn't expect it to last in the face of that sort of hammering. If he got me in the back, I'd spend the rest of my days in David Aston's cast-off wheelchair. If he got me in the head, the best I could hope for was that he'd kill me stone-dead.

As long as I stayed absolutely still and absolutely quiet, he seemed content to watch me carefully from those flicking white-rimmed eyes. As long as he didn't kick me again, I was content to lie there in the gutter, nursing my hurts and listening to the afternoon pass sunnily outside and waiting for someone to come. And hoping they would find us, because with the doors shut fast this stable looked like the other seven and I didn't dare call out for fear of what I might provoke. My best chance was that the horse might make a noise. Surely to God, he couldn't blame me for that?

I lay very still and very quiet and waited. The horse stood like a watchful statue at the door and waited too.

Outside someone got tired of waiting and started throwing stones onto the corrugated tin roof.

The horse's head jerked up as if he'd been shot, his eyes saucering wildly, his nostrils stretched. I had time only to think, "Oh no; oh please God, please Sally, no more," and then he was away, charging round the box, bouncing off the walls, his flying feet skidding on the corners, all that strength and energy under about as much intelligent control as a runaway train with no one in the cab.

Twice as the legs went from under him his big, angular body cannoned into me where I cringed in the corner. The second time, he regained his feet by thrusting off against my thigh. The edge of his hoof carved a deep gash in the unprotected flesh and I cried out, so he kicked me as well. Another stone landed on the roof and puttered tinkling down the slope to the guttering. The big horse crashed round his stable, almost screaming in his fear.

I began to lose track of what precisely was happening: whether he was running into me, or falling into me, or kicking me, or striking at me with his forefeet. I remember trying once to catch the lead rope that was flailing from his headcollar as he careered past, and he turned for a moment from his flight and reared over me, the hooves pawing way over my head. One of them struck my shoulder again as he came down and the pain was sickening. Such sense as there was in the scene began to fade, leaving a clattering chaos of fear and hurting and livid darkness.

Feeling my consciousness slipping, I did what I could to slump along the back wall, in the gutter, rather than out onto the floor in the path of those wild and crashing hooves.

But I didn't go out, not quite. I retained enough awareness to know that when the clattering stopped and the stable was suddenly flooded with light, it meant someone had opened the doors and the horse was gone. My first reaction was profound relief. My second was the fear that it was Sally come to finish me off.

The hands that straightened my body and lifted me were bigger than Sally's and gentle. I looked for a face and found Harry's, and he looked shocked and anxious and characteristically suspicious, as if I might have locked myself in a stable with a dangerous horse just to annoy him.

"What the *hell*—" he began, and there was a quiver in his deep voice.

"Oh, put me down," I said wearily. "It's all right. I'm all right."

We walked slowly into the yard. The sun hit me in the eyes. I kept his arm handy to lean on.

"What *happened?*"

I found a crumpled, unused handkerchief in his jacket pocket and held it over the congealing gash in my leg. "It was Sally."

His jaw dropped. "Sally Fane was here? When?"

I shook my head to indicate uncertainty. "Five, ten minutes ago? Not much more. She said she had a plane to catch."

"Jesus Christ!" He set off up the yard, towing me with him. "Come on, we're breaking in. Ellen will forgive us when she knows why I need her phone."

But Sally hadn't been gone ten minutes. She hadn't gone at all. She'd seen Harry coming up the drive—like me he'd left his car at home—and had ducked out of sight. She couldn't have expected this, but she was prepared for it: she must have left the rifle handy when she went to catch Gilgamesh.

And as we turned up the alley beside the byre, she was waiting in the upper yard with the gun at her shoulder. We stopped in our tracks. Harry raised one hand in warning.

"Sally—"

And she shot him in the chest.

V

After Bramham, when Gilgamesh and Lucy and the babies were turned out to grass and Pasha returned to Standings, the stables were given a last thorough clean-out and then the implements—

the barrow, the brooms, forks, and shovels—were stacked tidily against the wall of the stable block. As Harry clutched at himself with a grunt of surprise and then slowly subsided like a deflating balloon until he was half-sitting, half-lying on the concrete with his back against a stable door, I found myself reacting initially as neither a doctor nor a wife so much as a one-woman resistance army with something precious to defend. I looked round for something to fight with.

I was lucky on two counts. One was that among the heavy stable tools was a long-tined fork with a plastic handle, probably less sturdy for the job it was designed for but infinitely more wieldy for use as a weapon. Right then the chances of it surviving to be passed on to the Astons' heirs and assignees in forty years' time mattered less to me than the fact that, even in my bruised and battered condition, I could wield it without my arms dropping off.

And the other was that when Sally came round the corner after us, she came rifle first.

I swung the fork over my head, with the power of all the fear and fury and hatred within me and no regard for—in fact, no consciousness of—my own hurts, and the thing fell like an axe across the barrel, the steel shoulder hooking behind the gun and wrenching it out of her hands. Her cry was more startled than pained, but I had every hope that I had hurt her. If her finger had been through the trigger-guard, ready to fire again, I could have broken it.

The rifle clattered across the concrete and came to rest somewhere behind me, but I ignored it. I had a weapon I was effective with, and I wasn't turning my back on my enemy to exchange it for another I was less familiar with, which might anyway have been damaged by my attack. I followed the impetus of the fork round the corner, without giving Sally time to anticipate the move or myself time to think better of it, and found her standing there, somehow flat-footed, her hands apart. She was staring at them in surprise, as if she knew something had changed but hadn't yet worked out what, and a fraction of a second after I saw her, she saw me and her expression changed.

To fear. For the brief, glorious moment before she turned tail and ran, I looked into her eyes and saw that she was afraid. Sally Fane, who had the courage to ride the arrogant Gilgamesh at speed across fixed timber, who had the iron nerve necessary to plot and execute the means of wresting him from his owner, who had the cool command to lie low in her own house for weeks while the police combed the countryside for her and then come here with this parting gift for me before finally escaping the country and the pursuit. All that spoke of courage—of a strange kind, perhaps, but a high order.

And whatever happened next—whether she triumphed or justice did, whether she got clean away and made a comfortable new life for herself down the street from Ronnie Biggs, or was picked up and spent the next eight or ten years behind bars, and whether either Harry or I lived to see it—for that brief, glorious moment the sight of me lurching round the corner at her, bruised and bloody and pretty near mad with rage, whirling a stable fork as if in some esoteric eastern death ritual, struck sheer primitive fear into the very heart of her. If she had run away from nothing else in her life before, she ran away from me then. She thought I was ready to kill her, and the terror and helplessness of that, which she had already visited on me and Harry and David Aston, came home to roost.

And she was right. I could have killed her, even with that messy close-quarters weapon. When your back's against the wall, you can manage all sorts of actions not necessarily sanctioned by church and state. You do what you have to in order to survive, and your mind helps you out by tapping into some reservoir of atavistic passion, so that you actually want somebody wriggling bloodily on the tines of your fork. Great-great-aunt Wilma, with the bone through her nose and the nice line in mastodon cutlets, was in there swinging with me and would have joined me in a rousing cheer if the murderous weapon had connected with anything better than fresh air.

Wilma was out of luck. The murderous swipe was too long in the building: by the time it arrived, Sally had jumped back out of range, turned, and was pelting hell for leather up the top yard. With the gun on the ground behind me—ditto my husband—I pursued her only with a bellow of unusual volume and obscenity. Then I turned to see to Harry.

He wasn't dead. He wasn't even unconscious, but it was nasty enough. The hole was on the right side of his chest, two inches above the nipple, and the fact that it wasn't bleeding much on the outside was no guarantee that it wasn't bleeding inside. One lung seemed certain to be damaged, and the danger with that was not that he couldn't breathe adequately with the other but that air escaping from the punctured lung into the pleural cavity could force the collapse of the good one. The bullet hole should allow any such leakage to escape, but you couldn't be sure. Guns inflict notoriously unpredictable wounds.

In the old days, of course, when policemen all chain-smoked and were required to meet the stringent standards set by the Guild of Tobacco Processors before taking their sergeant's exam, he'd have had a cigarette-case in his breast pocket, ideally situated to deflect that bullet harmlessly into a stable door. So much for the Government Health Warning.

As I bent over him he cranked his eyes up to look at me, and there was shock and pain in his face, as well as that distinctive, indefinable something that made him Harry Marsh and no one else: a characteristic cocktail of fortitude and impatience, deep seriousness and wry self-mockery.

He said, "According to the police manual, that's not supposed to happen." His voice was soft and breathy, with a low murmur that could have been blood; but he didn't sound to me like a man at death's door.

A lump arrived suddenly in my throat and was only pushed down again by some determined blinking and swallowing. The biggest thing in my world just then was my desire not to lose him. "Shut up and lean forward."

That hurt, enough for his breath to catch and then hurry on laboriously, but he rested his forehead heavily on my aching shoulder while I checked his back for a second hole. There wasn't one; the bullet was still in his chest. The good news was that there was no exit wound four times the size of the entry pumping blood out of sight down the stable door.

He wasn't by any clinical assessment fit to be left, but I had no choice: he needed a ride to the hospital more than he needed my attentions. There was no prospect of a convenient passer-by, and anyway he wasn't going to come to much harm in the time it would take me to break Ellen's window and use her phone. Really the only thing that bothered me was that I didn't know where Sally had gone. She ought to have been heading for the rendezvous with her plane as fast as her athlete's legs could carry her, but we'd come unstuck before, trying to predict what Sally would do.

I retrieved the rifle and laid it across Harry's knees, pressing his hand over the stock. His attention was wandering. I spoke sharply to get it back. "Listen you. Stay awake for the next five minutes. If Sally Fane comes round that corner, put a hole in her. Also if that horse does. But if something short, dirty, and waving a bloody hanky does, hold your fire—it'll be me."

His fingers gripped mine with a kind of frail tenacity that was an echo of his sapped strength. "Be careful." Pain was beginning to chisel through the shock, tensing the facial muscles which had at first lain slack under the pallid skin. There was more stress in his breathing too.

I put his hand back on the rifle. "I'll take my trusty fork, and I'll be back before you know I've gone."

I went back to where it all began, jogging stiffly round the big, gently mouldering house to the study. The glass panes in the French window were small and not old, and when I broke one, I could make an aperture I could walk through instead of having to scramble. The way I felt, that mattered, but it would also be quicker. If I triggered the alarm, so much the better.

I never reached the phone. I broke the glass with the handle of the fork, reached carefully through to the latch, and pushed the window open. No alarm rang out, though it could have been one of those silent ones reporting to the local nick. And then, as I went to step inside, I sensed or saw—perhaps reflected in the glass as the French window swung open—an explosion of movement behind me, and instead of doing the intelligent thing, which would have been to dash inside, run upstairs, and lock myself in the bathroom, I turned round to see what it was.

It was Gilgamesh, still wearing nothing but a rope halter and a knotted rein, reunited with his crazed Valkyrie of a rider and coming at me like a cavalry charge. They must have come up the field while I was vandalizing Ellen's window, but I hadn't seen them until they were within a stride or two of the terrace. I just had time to thank God for the sheer four-foot rise from the field up to the paved promenade, which would keep the horse away from me even if it didn't deter Sally, and then they jumped it.

As the horse soared before me, filling all my vision with his great bulk and his fallen-angel grace, my mouth dropped open and I would most certainly have screamed if terror hadn't paralysed even that function. I thought I was dead. I thought there was nowhere for that horse to land except on me, and after that, they'd have trouble getting together enough bits for a decent funeral.

He had no intention of touching down on anything as squishy and insubstantial as a human being. The clatter of hooves on pavement was like a brief barrage of heavy artillery, then he had his feet under him and full control of his actions, and his shoulder, as he rocketed past, knocked me into the wall beside the French window and left me rolling in his wake across the terrace. I suppose that was when I lost the fork. I didn't see where it went and knew only that I was unarmed again.

Paving stones aren't like grass: the momentum of his passage took more killing when he couldn't dig his heels in and slide to a halt. The extra seconds it took Sally to rein him back and turn him gave me thinking space—not much, but all I was going to get. I had to get this right first time.

I could still get inside, but I'd get no chance to use the phone. I could probably lock myself where she couldn't get at me, but I could do nothing about summoning help from there. And if she couldn't get at me, she'd go down the yard and have another go at Harry. She knew he was injured. Since I hadn't got it, she probably knew he had the gun, but both of us knew his ability to use it at all accurately must be suspect. There was a strong possibility that he was lying there unconscious by now, in which case I had no doubt she would take the gun out of his limp hands and, helpless as he was, kill him with it. Even if he got off a shot first, there wasn't much prospect of him stopping her before she reached the gun. If she left me, it would be to kill my husband.

I was well below par myself, but I was a long way off helpless. I wasn't going to send her to Harry. I rolled away from the house, over the edge of the terrace.

She seemed to lose track of me for a moment then and rode back up the terrace and peered into the study. I crept quickly along the front of the house, hidden under the face of the retaining wall. I knew where I was heading, the one battlefield where I might have some kind of an edge, but it was a long way for someone on foot to keep ahead of someone on horseback and every inch of a head start I could manage was worth having.

With some regret I looked down the field to the fuchsia hedge enfolding my own house, but I couldn't go there. It was even further, she'd run me down half-way across the field, and if by any chance I made it, she'd come back for Harry. She had to follow me, and somehow I had to dispose of her. The only hope I had was in the wood.

I was just beginning to think I'd have to attract her attention when she spotted me. She let out a view halloo that struck chill to my heart, wheeled the horse in his own length, then clattered him across the terrace and dived him off onto the grass once more. The point of my concealing crouch gone, I abandoned it and bolted like a rabbit for my next covert, the sand school.

I reached the open gate with hot breath on the back of my neck and slammed it behind me. The horse pulled up short, and I swear there was disappointment in his long face. Sally's, in the brief moment that I saw it before she turned away, was aglow.

I knew, of course, that Gilgamesh could jump that gate. He'd done it before and nearly mowed me down that time too. In fact, I was hoping she would jump him into the school, because I was going out over the fence on the far side, which was higher. The fact that the rails were nicely spaced for climbing was no help to a horse, and the field gate was closed and set at an impossible angle for jumping.

I stood in the middle of the sand, surrounded by strange letters posted round the sides and bits of jumps piled in the corners, and tried to look scared and indecisive. Well, indecisive anyway: the other came naturally. I wanted her to think that I'd painted myself into a corner, had allowed her to push me in here and this was the end of my flight. If she thought that, she'd follow me inside. Then, while I scaled the fence, she'd have to either jump out again and work round via the terrace again or dismount to open the field gate. Whichever she did would earn me fifty yards of a head start. It wasn't nearly enough, but it was all I could think of.

For long seconds that I used to gasp some air into my lungs, Sally watched me over the gate, almost unblinking, considering the situation, assessing what I might do next. She appeared entirely to have forgotten the plane that was meeting her. She sat there so long and so still that I began to think she had dismissed the gate as impossible with neither saddle nor bridle and was wondering whether to come down and meet me on foot. I wondered how I should react if she did. Then, without warning, she clapped heels to the muscled flanks and set sail at the gate.

As soon as I saw she was committed, I turned my back on her and sprinted for the fence, springing at it out of my stride more like a ring-tailed lemur than a middle-aged writer with a bloody leg. It was an extravagant gesture, and it startled me at least as much as Sally, but it was the right move at the right time because a moment later the horse's shoulder cannoned off the rail immediately below my foot with all the velocity of his sprint and jump behind him. If he'd caught me, he'd have smashed my leg in pieces.

The fence shook with the impact as if it would fall under me. I didn't hang around to see: I was over the top rail and dropping down the far side, old bones and bruises notwithstanding, before it had made its mind up one way or the other. So it stood, for which I was grateful. If she could have ridden over it, she'd have ridden me down within a stride or two.

I think she did try to jump it, and I think the horse finally refused. Perhaps he could have done it: the fence was maybe a foot higher than the gate, pushing six feet, but nothing I had seen of him so far suggested he acknowledged limits to his ability. Maybe he was getting tired of being shoved around, scared, and yanked about and run into things, and with only a rope between them Sally couldn't compel his obedience. I heard her swearing behind me as I ran, but I didn't look back.

I ran with my fingers crossed. If he wouldn't jump the fence, maybe he wouldn't jump the gate again either, so whichever way she came she'd have to dismount. She could lead the horse through the field gate then, the shorter route, but she'd have to get on him again. It had to be worth time to me.

Many times since, I've walked along the hedge between the school and Foxford Wood, and wondered what the hell I was doing that I couldn't find some bolt-hole, if not into the wood itself then into the rough ground this side of it, in the time it took Sally to negotiate one gate or the other and get after me again. It was a doddle. Your arthritic granny could have done it.

But the truth was, I was tiring rapidly, the pummelling I'd already had from Gilgamesh was catching up on me, and even with my own safety and Harry's depending on it, I was running slower and slower, my feet held by invisible but ever more-viscid toffee. She was running me into the ground. Fight her? I wasn't going to stay on my feet long enough.

And now here they were again, racing over the turf behind me with a rumble like an orchestral climax. I couldn't hack it. The lungs were bursting out of me; my limbs were leaden and my head light. I was sobbing as I ran, only hoping that she couldn't hear. I could hardly hear it myself over the piston-hammering of my heart, and my tears were lost in the sweat that bathed me.

According to my mother, ploughboys sweat; gentlemen perspire, and ladies merely glow. Glowing enough to make a small desert bloom, wondering abstractly whether my heart or temporal artery would give way first, I ran on. When my legs wouldn't run any further, I walked; then I stopped, and after that, I sank to my knees. I was beaten and knew it. My only consolation, as I waited to be mauled, was that I'd brought her a fair way from Harry, and with any luck she wouldn't go back.

The horse stopped behind me. His shadow blotted out my sun. Still I waited, head bent—with exhaustion, not abjection, and I hoped she knew that—and nothing happened. At last, with my heartbeat easing up and my calves beginning to cramp, since one of us had to do something or we'd both die there of old age, I looked up.

There was absolutely nothing you could call an expression on Sally Fane's face. I got more response from eye-contact with the horse. It occurred to me that maybe her temporal artery had given way, but it wasn't a serious theory, more a forlorn hope. Right enough, at length she spoke.

"Is he dead?" There was no more feeling in her voice than in her face.

"Damn you." I began to cry. It wasn't a deliberate stratagem. I've never been the sort of woman who achieved anything by crying: I just look crumpled and dirty like one of Harry's handkerchiefs, so I do my best not to do it in company. I still think it was more down to tiredness than anything. But nothing I could have said at that juncture would have stood me in as good stead. If I'd lied, I believe she'd have known it. If I'd told the truth, God knows what she'd have done.

So I swore at her and began to cry, and finally she smiled quite gently and said, "There's just you, then."

VI

It was probably a mistake using the siren. There's not, after all, much point having a silent alarm if the police car responding to it can be heard coming a mile away. All the same, I was never so glad to hear something in all my life.

Sally, of course, heard it at the same moment. Anger flooded into her eyes. Even allowing for the stress she was under, the wild vacillation of her moods was extraordinary. She made mercury look phlegmatic.

She leaned down at me over the withers of the horse and hissed aspishly, "I thought you said he was dead." She managed to sound as if she was accusing me of something dreadful.

Actually I hadn't, but that was beside the point. "Harry didn't raise the alarm; I did. I opened the study window just before you knocked me off the terrace. It must be a silent alarm, reporting direct to the police station. I didn't know that."

"I did." Naturally; she would have made it her business to find out. "*Is* Harry dead?"

The squad car would be there in just a minute. There was no time for her to go back. "Not when I left him. But he wasn't up to making phone calls either." Actually I knew more than that, and I knew it without knowing how but with absolute certainty. I knew he was going to be all right. The load on me lightened. The hurts dulled, the bruises paled; even the weariness withdrew from the brink of utter exhaustion. The tears and the sweat were both drying on my cheeks.

I climbed to my feet. It was a slow, laborious climb, longer than I remembered it, and in the course of the final ascent I leaned my hand on the horse's kneecap with a familiarity that would have seemed incredible only a minute earlier, before we heard the siren. When I got there, I was closer, a little, to Sally's level. It seemed worth trying the woman-to-woman approach.

"Listen," I said. "I owe you nothing, not even good advice. But if it was me sitting there on top of an eventer, with a police car coming up the hill behind me and a get-away plane ready to fly me the hell out of here, I wouldn't be sitting there long. I'd be riding away at top speed, happy in the knowledge that where I led, no police vehicle in the world could follow, excepting only a helicopter and you have to book those three days in advance."

I could see her thinking about it. She glanced back at Foxford and then distantly at the wood as if her rendezvous with the expected plane was behind The Brink somewhere. On land at or convenient to Standings probably. There were any number of long, flat fields in the area where a light aircraft could land, and while several of them were currently knee-deep in growing barley, there was, in this horse-mad county, no shortage of pasture as well. "Where's he taking you?"

"Ireland," she said. Then a look of mingled slyness and outrage crossed her face, as if she'd caught me in some cunning subterfuge. Then she shrugged. "Well, they could guess that much—Harry's people." The way she said his name, all her problems were his fault. Even with his blood on her hands, she still hated him for it. "Then South America. I'm not telling you where. The place is full of stud-farms; a good English rider can always get work. I'll be all right." It wasn't me she was trying to reassure so much as herself.

What was keeping her? If she was waiting for me to wish her luck, she'd miss the plane.

"I don't want to go," she said, and smiled sadly. She sounded rather like a little girl leaving for her first Brownie camp and rather like a bride with the wedding car waiting at the door—not so much afraid of the future as clinging to the past. "I love this place."

If I'd had it in me to feel sorry for her, that would have been the time. I hadn't, but the time for hatred was gone too. "You could stay and sort it out."

"I'd go to prison!"

"Yes. But the time would get over, and then you could come back. From Bolivia or wherever, you'll never be free to come back."

She looked at me intently for a moment and then, straightening, turned and looked down The Brink onto Skipley, sprawling and grey and infinitely little in its dirty valley, compared with the rolling green and gold all round. She shook her head. "I couldn't bear to be confined. After this—this freedom, this power?

"You don't understand, do you? People who don't ride never do. You think it's something like keeping a cocker spaniel. Men think girls do it for the want of something between their legs. But it isn't sublimated mothering and it isn't sublimated sex: it's power, pure and simple. The Huns knew it. The Chinese, who lost one army and risked another to get horses, knew it. The Plains Indians knew it. David knows it—ask him. The strength and speed and endurance of the horse is something a man on foot can never match; but an unridden horse hasn't the courage to use its power. The combination of man and horse is greater than the sum of the parts.

"Well, I don't want to go back to being a mere human again. I won't be tied to the ground, like you. You might as well cut a runner's feet off, or a painter's hands. It's the same thing: deprive me of a horse and you cripple me. I won't live like that. I can *fly!* I will not be put in a cage!"

That was the root of all her problems, that feeling of being more than human, not bound by human rules and regulations, and she needed weaning off it as much as an alcoholic ever needed drying out. But I had no interest in her needs, not even enough to try to persuade her. She had hurt me too much. I wanted to get back to my husband and keep him safe and comfortable until the ambulance arrived.

I said, "Do what you like. I'm going back now." I turned away from her and began to trudge back across the field. I knew she could ride me down if she wanted. I didn't think she would. I was almost too tired to care. When I was half-way there the field gate swung open and a uniformed policeman shot through like a jack-in-the-box. He took two running strides towards me, hesitated on the third, then broke to a walk and stopped. I looked round, but Sally and the big bay horse were gone.

I got back to the yard just in time to see the ambulance disappearing down the drive. The policeman had radioed for it as soon as they'd found Harry, and it only had a mile to come.

"Damn," I said, angrily blinking back the tears I thought I'd seen the last of. "I wanted to go with him."

The policeman blinked too. He'd been looking at my thigh. I think it was the blood that fascinated him, though it could have been the sight of his superior's wife in a state of informality verging on undress. "Tell you what," he said. "Your house is just down the road, isn't it? If we drop you there, can you drive yourself down to the hospital? We'll have to take off after your friend on the horse, though God only knows where we'll find her."

I borrowed his map and indicated the line which Sally's gaze had sketched when she spoke of her escape. "Try along there. She's expecting a light plane to pick her up, so you're looking for a fairly big, flat field with nothing growing in it."

"Bless you, love," said his mate, his eyes warming, and we all piled into the squad car and zoomed backwards up the yard and then forward down the drive after the ambulance.

Fate spat in my eye again. At the end of the drive, when the driver throttled back to join the road, I heard the fractional waspish murmur above the car engine that said time was of the essence.

I glanced from one policeman to the other, but neither of them had heard it yet. In just a minute they could drop me at my door and go on from there. They wouldn't know when I'd first heard it. Harry needed me with him.

Harry would never forgive me if I let our needs interfere with

his job. I sighed wearily and announced, "I can hear the plane."
So we turned up the lane towards Standings.

It took eight minutes. Long before we raced round the curve of
the drive in front of Standings, spitting gravel at the Colonel's
windows, the little four-seater had dropped down over the mead-
ows towards Clayton, circled three or four times in preparation for
a landing, and vanished below the close and wooded horizon.

"Let me out here." I didn't want to be there when they caught
her—if they caught her, if it took longer to turn the plane and take
off again than it would take them to reach it. I could call a taxi
from the house; whatever role Colonel Fane had played, I didn't
think he'd begrudge me that. The car paused just long enough for
me to dive out and then hurtled on its way.

I went to the front door and rang the bell, but there was no
reply. The Fanes' housekeeper had left a week after Bramham;
now it was clear why. After Sally came back, they couldn't risk
having staff in the house. So I went to the back and knocked, and
when there was still no response, I tried the door and, finding it
unlocked, walked in. I didn't much like making free with the Colonel's house like this; but my need was pressing, and anyway, the
situation seemed to have passed beyond the point of normal cour-
tesy.

The telephone was in the hall, outside the sitting-room door.
The door was open, and as I passed, I saw the shape within of
Colonel Fane sitting in his preferred chair in front of the TV. He
gave no indication of being aware of my presence, but I didn't feel
I could help myself to his telephone without at least announcing
myself first.

I put one foot over the threshold and my head through the door.
"I'm just going to use your telephone, Colonel, if that's all right."

He looked round then—slowly, as if all his body had gone stiff.
The steel-blue eyes were expressionless, deep wells in which nothing moved. In the weeks since I had seen him, he had lost weight
and put on years. His face was drawn and harrowed into a relief
map of suffering. There was, too, a vacancy about him as if he'd

been left behind by events. He looked an old, old man waiting in his favourite chair for death or Meals on Wheels, whichever should come first.

His voice, when he spoke, was faint, as if it was already travelling across a greater distance than that between him and me. "Of course, Mrs. Marsh. Are you all right?"

"Yes. Thank you."

"I am glad," he said. "I tried to stop her, but . . ." He let the sentence peter out.

"She shot Harry."

"Oh no." I don't think I imagined the distress in his voice.

"I think he'll be all right. An ambulance took him to the hospital. I'd like to call a taxi and follow."

"Of course. No, take my car, it'll be quicker." He stood up and patted vaguely at his pockets. Then he shuffled over to the bureau and started opening drawers and feeling in pigeon-holes. I had never seen anyone outside a stroke ward move so slowly. I was beginning to think it would be quicker to call the taxi when he found them. "There. It's in the coach-house, round the corner in the straw yard. Take it. I shan't need it."

He held out his hand with the keys in the palm. I took the step or two into the room which were necessary to reach for them. As I took them, his hand closed on mine, firmly enough to startle yet somehow not to alarm me. It was a gesture almost of supplication.

"I really am most dreadfully sorry about what's happened," he said. "I hope you'll believe that I never knew anything of what she intended until after the harm was done. I could have given her up then, I suppose; but she is my daughter . . . But if I had, your husband wouldn't have been hurt. That at least is my fault. And the aircraft."

"The aircraft?"

"I heard it just now. I arranged that—arranged with a friend of mine for his son to pick her up and fly her to Ireland. He doesn't know the police are after her. He thinks they're going for a week-end's racing at Fairyhouse and then flying back. None of this is his fault."

Gently I extricated my hand. If I couldn't bring myself to free him from blame, neither did I feel any need to add to his burden. "I have to go. They'll be looking for me at the hospital."

"Of course. I'm sorry. I *am* sorry, about everything. I hope your husband will be all right."

I had a strong sense that he was saying goodbye. I hovered in the doorway, anxious to go and yet unwilling to leave him. I'd have felt less bound if he'd asked me to stay, felt less sympathy if he'd sought it. I knew that what he'd done and hadn't done had contributed to the train of events which left Harry lying in the dirt with a hole in his chest, but whatever the dictates of the law, it wasn't reasonable to expect him to have behaved in any other way. He had helped his daughter hide from her pursuers and had arranged to get her out of the country when the chance arose. He wasn't responsible for the hole in Harry's shirt.

I said, "Listen, this will all get sorted out. Whether the police pick up Sally or not. There'll be a lot of questions and a lot of fuss for a short time, and then gradually everything will start getting back to normal. I know how difficult it must be for you, but it won't go on being—forever, or even for very long. Stick with it; it'll get better."

He smiled then that sad, gentle smile that Sally had surprised me with. She was very like him. Sally's tragedy was that she had had no great cause in which to sink her energies and risk herself. Faced with an epic wrong, she would have triumphed spectacularly or, at worst, failed with honour. At Scutari she'd have been another Florence Nightingale; in the First World War, another Edith Cavell; in a storm-tossed rowing boat, another Grace Darling; at Mount Tabor, another Deborah. Sally's tragedy was that the only cause that came her way was her own success, the only great wrongs in her life the ones she wrought herself. If only she could have used the strength of purpose, the analytical mind, the skills and strategy she had learnt from her father in some way he could have been proud of. War would certainly have made her a heroine; without one, she'd had to devise her own.

Colonel Fane said, "I appreciate your kindness. I'm sorry I haven't done more to earn it. I really think you should go now, and see how Mr. Marsh is."

So I did, even though it was already in the back of my mind that I would never see him again. In that, however, I was wrong.

The straw yard to one side of the brick house marked the ancient demarcation line between estate and farm, between owners and workers, landscape and land. It was where the ricks had once stood, in the days before combine harvesters and Dutch barns and now the pieces of farm machinery stood there, waiting for their turn to come round with the seasons. Between the ploughs and harrows and reapers and rakes, a fairway had been left to the coach-house where the cars were kept. I walked towards the door up this avenue of machinery like a farmer's bride, lacking only the arch of crossed pitchforks and a muck-spreader for the drive to the reception.

And then it was as if a careless step had taken me across the invisible, fluctuating boundary of a time-warp and I was flipped back down the progression of my own hours, because long before I reached the door, hemmed in as I was by walls of agricultural equipment whose purposes I could mostly only guess, I heard again the hollow, rhythmical step which had filled me with such irrational terror—well, at that stage it was irrational—in the stable yard at Foxford.

There were of course differences. This time I knew she was there and she didn't know I was. The horse's stride was freer now she wasn't holding him back to stretch the moments and savour the mounting tension. And we weren't the only people on the place: Sally was calling to her father as she rode up the yard.

"Daddy? I didn't go. When it came to it, I couldn't. I don't want to spend the rest of my life in Brazil! I wouldn't have made it, anyway: there's a police car down on the forty-acre; I expect when they realise I'm not going to show, they'll come up here. Daddy, I want—"

A full half-minute must have passed from when I first heard her to when she turned the corner of the straw yard and saw me. I could have used that time, to run silently on moccasined feet and let myself into the coach-house out of sight or just to get in among the bulky big machines and duck down. Either would have served, but I managed neither. I froze—like a climber on a rockface or a linesman up a pole or a rabbit fixed in the murderous unwinking stare of a stoat. Fear rooted me to the spot, the impossible fear of something I had already faced and survived, which even malicious fate couldn't ask me to face again. Mixed with the fear were incredulity and outrage, but they didn't help my feet unstick from the concrete until it was already too late.

I'm not sure Sally wasn't more shocked than I was. The last thing she had expected to find here was me. She had left me behind, not only physically but in her mind and memory, when she went to meet her plane. Somewhere along the way she had changed her mind about accepting exile; I'm still not sure what she intended doing instead, but she had ridden back home, knowing the police were no distance behind her, to tell her father of her decision. And there, in her own back yard, ready to intrude even on that brief, emotional, infinitely private moment, she found me.

Through no choice of mine, I had come to wear the face of Nemesis for Sally Fane. It must have seemed to her that whenever her options narrowed, when opportunity slammed a door on her and luck ripped the rug from under her feet, I was there. I hadn't engineered her downfall, though I had made my contribution to the process. But I think that by being there at every turn, watching her dream turning to ashes and occasionally giving the ashes a little stir, I had become associated in her mind with the terrible price she was going to have to pay for losing her gamble on Gilgamesh. That was what the ambush at Foxford had been about. Before she left, she wanted to erase me—negate me, demolish me, rub me out.

And now, this late in the game, here I was again, witnessing her ultimate defeat. It was the last straw and I saw it break her reason. I saw rage burst like a storm in her eyes, filling them with darkness. I saw her face twist up with fury as if at an injustice, and the darkness of blood suffuse it. I saw her mouth gape with anger and heard a sound like mayhem ripping out.

And then she turned the horse by the rope along his neck and drove her heels into his muscled flanks, and he exploded into action, a roll of thunder and vengeance hurtling down on me head-on, so that almost all I was aware of was the wideness of his eyes, the flare of his nostrils, and the piston-pounding of his knees as they shot half-way up his chest with every stride.

Everything after that happened so incredibly quickly that you couldn't split the separate events away from the fast, hard core of time driving through them. But for me on the inside it was somehow different: there *was* time to take account of the moment's component parts, almost as if the horse galloped in slow motion. I could watch his knees raking up and his neck thrusting out with the effort of acceleration. I could see the madness in the face of the rider crouched over his shoulder. I could feel the slow percussion in my ankles as I ran backwards, each awkward step taking long moments and leaving me out of contact with the earth for far too long. And I felt the shock, short of pain but high on comprehension, as my career backwards came to an abrupt end on the sprung tines of a hay-rake.

I don't know if Sally knew it was there at the end of the avenue and was deliberately driving me onto it, if she knew it was there and didn't care, or whether in her rage she hadn't even seen it. But as soon as I felt its sharp prod through my shirt, I knew what it was and what it meant, and the consequences for all three of us if she didn't rein the horse back right now. If she hit me travelling at that speed, the tines would transfix me. Then the horse would run them deep into his chest. And if that happened Sally would fly forward onto the rows of spines like a battery of Catherine wheels.

I opened my mouth to warn her, but all that came out was a scream.

Then from somewhere behind the horse, just audible over the clamour of his hooves, a single shot rang out. Sally straightened abruptly out of her crouch, surprise registering in her face in the moment before she fell.

Unbalanced by the loss of his rider, freed from her hand and heels, the horse swung away from me and towards the coach-house door where he pulled up, stamping and blowing, sweat lathering his coat.

I eased forward the fraction necessary to take the hooks of the rake out of my skin, then less cautiously the extra inches that freed them from my shirt. I looked at the horse, but without his taskmaster he was no danger to me.

I looked at Sally. The rifle bullet had passed clean through her shoulder and should not have imperilled her life; but the plough she had fallen on had broken her neck and she was already dead. No more rides for this Valkyrie.

And I looked back up the straw yard towards the side of the house in time to see the back door close on the figure of the Colonel, beating his last retreat. I stood and waited. I knew what he was going to do. I knew why he had had the gun out and loaded at so fortuitous a moment. All he needed now was a few moments to reload.

The second shot came just as the police car raced into the yard.

VII

David understood it best of anybody.

We finally had our meal together, the four of us: OK, so it was a Chinese take-away, in tinfoil boxes with plastic chopsticks, and we ate it on the verandah of Skipley General Hospital while the sun went down over Foxford Wood, but with David still mostly in a wheelchair and Harry trussed up like a Christmas turkey, we wouldn't have got in anywhere more salubrious.

We ate and drank rice wine, and watched the sunset, and eventually, inevitably, the conversation turned quietly onto Sally Fane and her burning desire, finally fulfilled, though not as she had intended, to stamp her name on the public consciousness. And it was not Harry, with his policeman's experience of strained and savage people, or me, with my intuitive imagination, but David Aston who could make most sense of what had happened.

"It's hard for anyone outside to appreciate the pressures involved in professional sport—by which I mean all sport which is the athlete's sole or major occupation. There are pressures in every business, I know, but sport is unique on a number of counts. Firstly, sportsmen are usually entering their highest level of competition when their emotional maturity is at its lowest ebb, in the late teens and early twenties. Those are bad years for taking sensible decisions. Then, too, to be in with a chance of making the big time, the kid with potential has to be spotted early and encouraged to focus all his energies on this one area of his life. It's the only way to succeed, but it doesn't make for a well-rounded human being.

"By the time he's twenty-one the typical athlete has eaten, breathed, and slept his sport day and daily for ten, even fifteen years. The only friends he has live the same way; the only authority he's been taught to respect is his coach. Otherwise rules are for bending, records are for breaking, and the sheer physical limitations of his body are something he's taught to push against as hard as he can. Winning is what counts: nobody gives a tinker's how you play the game. And around twenty-one you're probably winning at the highest level you'll achieve. There are exceptions—eventing is one, though you don't find many people still competing in middle age—but for the most part sport is a young person's business. Old sportsmen never die; they just get beaten more and more soundly until they crawl off and start boring barmen. Age isn't an accomplishment in sport; it's a disaster.

"By the time he's twenty-five, sooner in some sports, he's having to run faster than ever just to stay in the same place. Kids of seventeen are coming up and pushing him, and he knows damn well that anything he's going to do in this world he's been taught to consider the only important one has to be soon, because the longer it takes, the harder it's going to be. If he isn't close by now, he might as well go home. If he is close, he's going to pull out every stop he can reach—mental, physical, emotional, and sometimes criminal—to get there. It's his last chance to make all the work and all the hurting worthwhile.

"That's when it happens. The last inhibitions go, the ones that keep you alive and just about sane. Riders ride on when they know they're injured. Boxers cover up conditions the Board of Control would lift their licences for. Track athletes start packing their own blood. The drugs bill goes up, and there are more on the menu: steroids for strength, bute for pain, uppers for performance, downers to relax. They get caught, but not all of them and not at once. The prize is worth the risk. For them there won't always be another shot at it.

"What I'm saying is that if sportsmen go crazy sometimes, it's not all their own fault. You can't take a kid of seven or eight and spend fifteen years telling him that what he does is the most important thing in the world, and telling him to swallow the pain and the exhaustion it costs him, and telling him he can be the greatest if he'll only push himself to the limit, and then not deliver, and still have a mature, emotionally balanced young man capable of coping with that disappointment and moving on from it. It's natural to admire excellence, but if you make a fetish of it—and whether you like it or not, it's not only sportsmen but our society which does that—then you're creating a religion that demands human sacrifices."

The rice wine went round again.

Harry shrugged lopsidedly, since one shoulder still couldn't move too far. All the same, he was looking much better. He was beginning to crumple again round the edges. The week he'd been in bed, white bedclothes stretched too taut and too smooth over his bulky frame, his face smooth and white to match, he'd hardly seemed the man I married at all. The breakthrough on the road to recovery came when the nurses let him feed himself, and reassuring blobs of tomato sauce and strawberry jam started appearing on his pyjamas. The first time I came through the door to be met by a large pink stain like a map of India, I knew we were out of the wood.

He said, "Even if that's all true, as it may well be, it isn't relevant. OK, it's another reason why someone might break the law. Add it to the list; there's never a shortage of reasons. Every crime ever committed had a reason; most of them had several. What interests me is not what reason a criminal gives for his action, but why he lacks the inhibitors that stop the rest of us from responding to our problems with violence. No crime was ever committed for a reason that didn't apply equally to a whole lot of other people who didn't murder their grannies or rape the charlady in consequence.

"Perhaps particularly as a policeman but also as a member of society—who has never, incidentally, shared the view of sportsmen that what they do is important—I don't very much care why crimes are committed. No, not quite: I want to know if anybody's hungry enough to steal food. That's probably the only crime for which society is responsible. Is it society's fault if a minority of people want to spend more money than they make, crave drugs or fast cars, can't cope with the normal irritations of human relationships without resorting to violence? I don't believe it is, and I don't believe it can do anything but harm to suggest that people are not fundamentally responsible for their own actions.

"All through our lives, all of us flirt briefly with unlawful responses to our dilemmas. We don't turn that momentary contemplation into action for one of two reasons: we're afraid of getting caught, or we accept that the thing is wrong. Sociologists would achieve more lasting good if they abandoned their research into the multifarious reasons for crime and worked at reinforcing that concept of wrong which they've spent the last twenty years trying to erase.

"I suppose," he added acerbically, as a side-swipe at me, "that's too simple for the creative thinkers among us."

"Too simple," I agreed, "or at least too simplistic. And anyway no help in resolving a situation. As long as you refuse to consider motivation, you can only ever respond to a crime, not act to prevent it. You can fill the prisons that way and do wonders for your clear-up statistics, but you can't prevent any of the human misery locked up in those figures.

"Your problem is that you can't discriminate between understanding a crime and condoning it. The fact that David can trace the chain of consequences that led to Sally's actions doesn't make him any more likely to repeat them than you are. But it does make him more likely to spot it in time if he ever sees it happening again, and maybe he could stop it, whereas the best you could do would be an early arrest. Two people died and two were seriously injured because of what took place in Sally's mind. If someone had foreseen it, all that could have been prevented. Medicine isn't the only field in which prevention is better than cure."

After another orbit by the wine Ellen, who had sat there almost in silence while we discussed the criminal as victim, as jail-bait, and as an intellectual conundrum, offered her view. She made no pretentions to great erudition, nor was she a religious woman. She was asked, by Harry in fact, for her opinion as a representative of the great mass of right-thinking people, not exactly an unbiased observer but someone without a direct involvement in sport, law enforcement, or crime, and she gave it.

"What I don't understand," she said quietly, "is how we can have this discussion—we four people, in precisely these surroundings and circumstances—and we can consider what Sally did, and why, and how the responsibility breaks up; and we can talk about it at length without anybody saying the word 'evil.' We can debate the shooting of two unarmed men as an aberrant response to stress, or a criminal act facilitated by the failure of natural inhibitions, or a social problem to be defined, even if it can't be resolved;

and not one of you, not even you, Harry, is prepared to commit yourself to a judgement.

"You want to know what the great mass of right-thinking people might say about this? In my opinion, they would say that what Sally did was wicked. Anything else is secondary to that. All that is necessary for evil to prosper is for good men to discuss psychology."

The wine was finished. So was the sunset. We turned a little on the verandah to watch the stars emerge twinkling from the deepening dark over Skipley.

Harry said, "Then what about the Colonel? Was he a victim or a perpetrator?"

I shook my head. "He saved my life, I'm not qualified to judge. I do know, for what it's worth, that he considered himself culpable —not so much for the attack on you, David, of which he had no knowledge and no suspicions until we planted them, as for what she did to Harry and tried to do to me. That wouldn't have happened if he hadn't sheltered her. That was why he was always going to kill himself as soon as she was gone, one way or another."

Harry gave a pensive sniff. "In that moment when he saw what was happening and turned his gun on her, I wonder what was going through his mind. That this was something he had to do to save you? That shooting Sally would save you, while shooting you wouldn't save her? Or was it a punishment for what she'd done, not least to him, and saving you was only the acceptable face of vengeance?" He shrugged again, off-centre. "I don't know. He was an honourable man, but he was a ruthless one too, in his way."

David cleared his throat very quietly; still all our eyes turned to him. He knew the answer to Harry's question. Apart from the opening scene, he'd been present for none of the drama; yet we who had seen it through from curtain to curtain could only speculate, while David knew.

"Breeding horses is a kind of sport too. Gilgamesh was the triumph of his skill, the horse he wanted to be remembered by. If he'd done nothing, Sally would have killed Gilgamesh as surely as she'd have killed Clio and herself. He couldn't do anything to save Sally. So he saved the horse."

In the night sky the constellation of Pegasus began to climb.

JO BANNISTER, a successful writer and newspaper editor in Northern Ireland, has won several awards for journalism in the United Kingdom, including the Royal Society of Arts bronze medal. She is the author of six previous novels. *Gilgamesh* is her fourth for the Crime Club.